THE QUEST

Vinod Nair was born in New Delhi and graduated in B.Com from Delhi University. He went on to complete his study in International Management from the Chartered Management Institute (UK). He has lived in New Delhi and Gurugram for over forty years and his fascination with the city has seen him write his second book after the very successful release of his first book *Delhi OMG*.

Vinod stays in Ohio (USA) with his wife and daughter Carissa.

THE QUEST

VINOD NAIR

Om Books International

First published in 2025 by

Om Books International

Corporate & Editorial Office
A-12, Sector 64, Noida 201 301
Uttar Pradesh, India
Phone: +91 120 477 4100
Email: editorial@ombooks.com
Website: www.ombooksinternational.com

Sales Office
107, Ansari Road, Darya Ganj,
New Delhi 110 002, India
Phone: +91 11 4000 9000
Email: sales@ombooks.com
Website: www.ombooks.com

ISBN: 978-93-6395-625-4

Printed in India

10 9 8 7 6 5 4 3 2 1

Dedicated to the discovery of ourselves and the journey towards finding our sense of purpose. May we never stop exploring who we are and who we are meant to be.

The more you live
The less you die...
Janis Joplin

PROLOGUE

She possessed an intriguing blend of authenticity and innocence—an unusual mixture for someone whose livelihood depended on navigating a world of forced submission, often on a nightly, if not hourly, basis. In the dimly lit quarters where she spent her evenings, there were moments when the submissiveness was not merely a product of force but a response to overwhelming circumstances. Here, she faced the formidable challenge of surrendering to the desires of a group of men who were insidiously marketed to her by her 'madam,' each encounter a delicate dance between compliance and survival.

On the other hand, I was far from a typical customer and had no intentions of becoming one. My participation in this escapade was spurred on by the urging of friends, who painted a picture of a fun-filled night out that transcended the ordinary.

"Come on, let's have some fun. We'll grab some drinks and check into a hotel room, and I know someone who can arrange exactly what we desire." His curiosity was piqued as he questioned the nature of their desires.

Abhay, a key figure in the group, continued to outline our plans. "We'll get our drinks, head to Al Kauser, have some kebabs, and then reach out to my buddy for an after-party. Who is up for it?"

"We are all here for a good time. There will be no trouble, I hope," I said.

"You are such a fattu yaar. Nothing will happen. Big brother is here." The group burst out laughing, wasting no time. "Who is up for it?"

The casual progression of the plans did not reveal what the future had in store for our motley group of friends out to have a good time. Our group, with contrasting personalities, was unaware that the night was going to reveal its true colors soon. The air crackled with the palpable energy of anticipation. Hands shot up in unanimous agreement, yet I found myself caught in a moment of introspective hesitation.

I so wanted to escape from all this and not be thrust into this world which demanded participation to be considered relevant. I thought again and then reluctantly raised my hand to be counted with the rest. Some were surprised, some did not care, and some just did not notice.

Laughter echoed in the car as our group drove towards Al Kauser at Sardar Patel Marg, with the infectious beats of Honey Singh and Badshah reverberating through the inadequately equipped 1000-watt speakers of our Hyundai Accent. The joyride was quickly cut short as we narrowly missed a disinterested traffic police officer during an audacious U-turn onto the road leading to Al Kauser. This brief encounter with authority, a mere blip in our plans, emboldened us, knowing that a short distance lay between us and the intoxicating blend of meat and alcohol.

The car's hood became a makeshift dining table, with an assortment of kebabs and biryani. Amidst this exhibition of gluttony, the conversations ranged from politics to spirited debates about movies and the school and college romances that had died a quick death.

Abruptly, the arrival of a police car signaled a potential disruption. Panic surged within me as I thought of what I had asked earlier: "There will be no trouble, I hope." Why had I agreed to be part of this madness?

"Oye!" the police officer exclaimed. "What's going on? Alcohol consumption in a public place is prohibited, and you are all going to spend the night in jail."

Seizing the initiative, Manoj, with his street-smart demeanor, emerged as the de facto negotiator. The others in the group—myself and two friends from Delhi—found ourselves ill-equipped for this unforeseen encounter.

Manoj took the constable aside and was soon engaged in a conversation which the rest of the group knew nothing about. Observing from a distance, we witnessed Manoj skillfully guiding the police officer towards a secluded section of the parking lot. There was a shake of hands, and, in the end, they returned to the car as if they were long-lost friends. The police officer now had a smile on his face as he offered a word of caution to the group: "Be careful, and don't drink and drive."

Nods of acknowledgment followed, and the animated exchange resumed almost as if nothing had happened.

The group continued to gorge on the kebabs, garnished with generous servings of onion and tomato slices sprinkled with chaat masala. When the clock had ticked past 11 PM, a collective decision was made to proceed with the next phase of our audacious plan. Abhay, always the orchestrator, initiated a phone call to his contact—the individual responsible for the remaining part of the agenda. There lingered an air of uncertainty in Abhay's voice as he dialed the number, though he assured the group, "I'm not sure if they are available, boss, but he never disappoints."

As Abhay distanced himself from us for his clandestine negotiation, it was evident that a discreet conversation was underway. Ten minutes later, he rejoined the group, triumphantly declaring, "It's done. We need to wait in the lobby. Two of them will be available at 10,000 rupees per person. I have already agreed. Come on, it's not much for a good night."

The group collectively voiced their agreement, yet Manoj and I remained silent. The cost, in our eyes, did not seem extravagant, yet this was not something that we could commit to. At a basic level, it did not seem right.

Returning to the hotel, Abhay and Sunil completed their check-in, drawing a puzzled expression from the receptionist at the conspicuous absence of luggage. Meanwhile, Manoj and I chose to distance ourselves from the unfolding madness, opting to leave the duo behind. The quintessential Delhiites, armed with financial means, influence, and an abundance of vices, navigated situations that seemed to come naturally to them with the solutions in tow.

As Abhay and Sunil stepped into the elevator for their hotel room, a parting gesture left us in fits of laughter. The two friends, inebriated but unfazed, waved and blew kisses in our direction. We stayed in the lobby for a while, seeking solace in a glass of water as we attempted to regain our senses. This pause was deemed necessary before embarking on the lengthy journey back home.

Throughout this entire sequence of events, a lingering sense of foreboding had accompanied me, an unshakable feeling that something would go awry. Little did I know that this premonition would prove accurate, but the unfolding drama would take an entirely unexpected turn.

It began with the arrival of two young women who walked through the entrance, immersed in an animated conversation.

My attention was diverted as I perched on a large wing chair, facing the opposite direction. It was Manoj who subtly gestured for me to look behind, stating under his breath, "That's them."

Intrigued, I inquired, "How can you tell?" while still staring at Manoj.

"Two of them," Manoj explained, "one in red, another in black, just as Abhay described."

I turned to look, and it was at that moment that I was confronted by a sight that filled me with shock and disbelief.

"Oh my God," I nearly exclaimed aloud, "this can't be true. Oh my God, is that not…?"

The Past

Chapter 1

In the mad dash to the bus stop, the thrill of possibly getting a seat next to one of the girls from the neighboring school added a jolt of excitement to every step. Backpacks felt heavier with all the unspoken hopes and dreams of a quick glance or a shy 'hello'. Most days, though, the courage ran out before the words even started. Still, despite the awkward pauses and missed chances, the audacity of hope stayed strong, giving each morning a hint of romance—or our interpretation of it.

En route to the bus stop, a lively procession of students from the all-boys school unfolded. Some dragged their feet as they forced themselves to move forward, others hopelessly protested the early hour, and a few embraced the journey with cheerfulness. I belonged to the indifferent lot, blissful in the thought that no matter what one feels or says, the journey had to be undertaken. I termed it as indentured servitude. This daily ritual was always punctuated by a momentary pause at an intersection. This was the last visual connection with home, and an earnest gaze anticipating the routine wave from my father. The wave, a silent farewell, initiated the continuation of my long walk to the bus stop. Over time, the casual wave, however fleeting, remained etched in my mind only to be reignited many years later over a more tragic circumstance.

In the event of a delayed bus, the wishes for an unplanned holiday emerged, guilt-free and shared with the missed companionship of the neighboring girls. Those instances of missed buses translated into days filled with endless rounds of random cricket matches on any patch of land on which a ball could bounce. The very fabric of these "Type 4" government accommodations where I resided held a peculiar charm. A large rectangular patch of land separated two row houses. They weren't architectural marvels but served the purpose of enabling impromptu cricket matches and broken window panes.

Contrasting with the modest government accommodations, the opulence of the 'main road-facing' houses and bungalows in Shalimar Bagh, Punjabi Bagh, and other parts of West Delhi became apparent. Some of these houses, with names like 'Apni Kutiya' or 'My Humble Cottage,' exhibited an audacious attempt at masking snobbery with humility.

The government flats, single-storeyed townhouse structures, boasted expansive rooftops shared by occupants on the ground and first floors alike. These rooftops served as multifunctional spaces—the Punjabi aunty drying her oversized bra on a clothesline adorned with more colorful clips than a rainbow, to homemade papad and 'vadiya' laid out on a charpoy for drying, and the rhythmic knitting marathons that unfolded with the grace of a pianist. Each rooftop told a unique story. For me, the rooftop became the venue to release kites effortlessly during the months of July and August or the arena for spirited games of mini hand cricket—a haven of simple joys amid the suburban landscape.

As someone with South Indian roots, commonly referred to as a 'Madrasi' by the bullies, I found solace within a small group of three friends. Despite being a diligent student, I rejected the conventional teenage rebelliousness, earning the tag of a 'boring and studious' boy.

My actions were always fueled by motivation and the expectation of a reward. The trips to the school bus stop were driven by the expectation of meeting girls from the neighboring school, and my desire to gain mastery of the English language was due, in large part, to my infatuation with my English teacher.

She would sashay into the class in her saree, and my heart would skip a beat. I delved into Shakespeare and his works, recited Keats and Byron effortlessly, and basked in the praise she showered on me, which only deepened my belief in the unthinkable.

One day, after class, she stopped me. "You have a remarkable way with words," she said, her voice warm and encouraging. "Have you ever considered writing something of your own?"

Caught off guard, I stammered, "I—I don't know if I'm ready for that."

Her smile lingered. "Start small. Even a single line of your own can carry more meaning than a hundred lines borrowed from others."

Her words lingered with me, fueling both my admiration and a tiny spark of hope.

Despite my earnest efforts to impress her, I realized they never extended beyond the English period. I understood that some dreams, no matter how fervently imagined, remain trapped in the realm of illusions. At that moment, the theory of manifestation made no sense to me.

"What was I thinking?!"

As school gave way to college, the juncture of decision-making about my life's trajectory arrived. While classmates like Abhay and Sunil seamlessly integrated into family businesses, for me and my two companions, the journey to determine our destinies was just beginning.

"It seems like everyone around us is already set on their paths, but I feel like I'm still figuring things out," I confided in Abhay during one of our evenings together.

"I understand, yaar. It can be pretty overwhelming, especially when it feels like everyone else has it all figured out. Trust me, a lot of people are still figuring things out too; they just might not show it."

Sunil interjected, "Exactly. We're all on our own journeys, and honestly, college is the best time to experiment and explore what really gets you excited."

"I know, but it's hard not to compare, you know? Seeing you guys step so easily into your family businesses… sometimes it feels like I'm just falling behind."

Abhay leaned forward, shaking his head. "It's not as simple as it looks, bro. Just because we're walking into something set up for us doesn't mean it's all smooth sailing. We've got our own challenges, and the pressure—it's real."

Sunil nodded, jumping back in. "Look, you've got your own path, and that's a good thing. Keep an open mind. Life's unpredictable. Anything can happen."

As future events unfolded, truer words had never been spoken. The worst, as it turned out, had only just begun.

As my friends prepared to chase their dreams abroad, I, the supposed 'boring student,' embarked on a divergent path. Choosing to work with Altos India Ltd., I concurrently decided to dabble in French and enrolled in French classes at Alliance Française de Delhi. Simultaneously, evening classes were dedicated to pursuing an MBA, a fashionable trend of the time.

The multiple areas that I had spread myself into—with French classes in South Extension in the morning, work in Greater Kailash II, and MBA courses in Pushp Vihar near Saket in the evening—took a toll on my physical appearance. The unpredictability of public transport, with its crowded buses and ensuing stampede, left me arriving at work with crumpled attire and shoes that bore the imprints of countless footfalls. The mixture of my sweat and the collective odor of unwelcome fellow commuters rubbing cheek-to-jowl with me during my commute left me wondering if this was going to be the state of my future. If my struggles were going to be imprinted in my daily life in this manner.

Determined to change things up, I bought myself a bike—a Kawasaki Bajaj. It wasn't just a ride; it was a badge of pride. I'd scraped together the down payment after months of pinching pennies, wanting to keep this one free from any help from my parents. Living at home with my parents meant I could save faster, bringing that dream a little closer. Soon, the bike was more than just wheels—it was my trusty sidekick, getting me from French classes to work, then to MBA sessions, and finally back home at the end of a long, satisfying day.

After my father's retirement from government services, the once familiar Type 4 government flat in Netaji Nagar became an empty shell, a temporary refuge that I could inhabit for up to three months post his departure. The absence of rent was a saving grace, considering the meager salary I earned at that time.

The solitude of those walls marked the entrance of Indrani, a captivating Bengali woman who had recently joined Altos India as a Senior Business Analyst.

Indrani was more than just beautiful; she was fiercely ambitious. From the start, her sharp, focused gaze and relentless work ethic made it clear she was driven by an unquenchable thirst for success. Every project was a calculated step toward her ultimate goal, and she thrived in the competitive environment, turning challenges into showcases of her strategic skill. For Indrani, climbing the corporate ladder wasn't just a goal—it was about reaching heights few dared to dream of.

In the private sphere, away from the boardrooms and the bustling offices, I glimpsed a side of Indrani that few others had the privilege to see. There, her ambition burned just as fiercely, if not more so, than in her professional pursuits. Whenever we met, there was an allure that I found hard to ignore. It was hiding in plain sight. Our conversations often revolved around dreams and aspirations. Whether discussing future plans or reflecting on past achievements, her eyes sparkled with an unwavering determination.

She navigated office politics with a finesse that bordered on ruthlessness. Colleagues spoke in hushed tones about her ability to outmaneuver any opposition, her determination to rise above the constraints that others accepted as inevitable. Most could tell that she was destined to rise far beyond what lay before her as part of a regular career progression. None of us had an inkling of the depths she could stoop to or the heights she could aspire to.

When her real intent became obvious, it just blew me away.

As colleagues, we bonded initially over shared projects and late-night brainstorming sessions. Our friendship deepened steadily, and I began to notice a subtle undercurrent of attraction between us. Office hours turned into moments of stolen glances, and our shared laughter during coffee breaks reflected a connection that both exhilarated and intimidated me.

Her eyes were alluring, and her husky voice had an inviting quality that I found hard to resist. It seemed strangely seductive, even as I struggled to maintain the line between professional decorum and personal desires. Despite my resolve, I found it to be a losing battle, and it wasn't long before I found myself surrendering to feelings that grew stronger with each passing moment.

The muted glow of the office lights spilled into the late hours as Indrani and I found ourselves engrossed in numerous conversations that went beyond the limits of project timelines and corporate strategies. Indrani's eyes, usually sharp and focused, softened as she spoke about her dreams and aspirations, laying bare the layers that lay closely guarded beneath her fiercely ambitious exterior.

"Doesn't life in Netaji Nagar feel like a distant memory compared to the whirlwind of this corporate world?" she said, half-smirking.

I smiled. "It sure does. But there's more to life than just climbing the corporate ladder, don't you think?"

Indrani's laughter echoed in the quiet office space.

"You might be onto something there. Sometimes, I wonder what it would be like to break free from these shackles, explore the uncharted territories of life."

I was intrigued. "Maybe it's time to find out. Life is too short for regrets."

"You know, there's something about these late nights that makes everything feel more ... authentic."

I nodded in agreement.

The silence that followed spoke volumes, pregnant with unspoken possibilities. The illusion of romance danced in the spaces between our words, with each one desiring the other to make the first move.

I let the feeling of something deeper pass and instinctively stood up, signaling that it was time to leave. She stared at me as her lips curved into a smile and held out her hand. I took it and helped her up, her fingers clenching my hand in a strong, warm grip.

Something did not seem right—or was it my in-built aversion to taking risks coming to the fore?

As the days progressed, the work pressures kept me late in the office longer than I would have liked. Strangely, once everybody had left, my eyes would inadvertently search for Indrani. On some occasions, I would spot her near the coffee vending machine, and on other occasions, hard at work at her workstation. A wave or a smile evinced a reciprocal response from me. I was careful not to let my perceived sense of affinity become the subject of office gossip and so cleverly camouflaged it under the garb of a good office working relationship. There was more to it, as I began to feel, the undercurrents fairly evident. I had noticed that she was not keeping late hours anymore, and although I wanted to quiz her about it, the opportunity did not present itself.

A week passed, and one day I was getting ready to leave after a busy day at work. It was almost 7 PM when I heard a voice over my shoulder.

"Somebody is really working hard nowadays."

I turned back, half-startled. It was Indrani. I laughed awkwardly and responded, "Work comes in the way of relaxing days."

"Want to grab some dinner?" she asked. "I am starving, and I hate to eat alone."

"Sure," I said. "Give me a second to wrap up my stuff."

"Sure, no rush," she replied as she looked at her cellphone and furiously ran her fingers over the screen, texting someone.

A minute later, we were heading toward the parking lot.

"Should we head to the Smokehouse Grill?" I asked. "It's nearby, and since you are starving…".

"Sounds perfect," she replied, still looking at her phone.

Once we reached the restaurant, we were ushered to a great spot that ensured a fair degree of privacy without too much human traffic or noise—a nice, quiet corner.

We continued to chat on a wide range of topics. I couldn't help but feel that she appeared a trifle distracted, almost as if there was something on her mind that she wanted to share but couldn't. Both of us spoke about work, politics, future goals, and shared a few laughs. I was beginning to feel very relaxed in her company and was really enjoying the evening.

It was time to leave, and then she asked if I would like to drop in for some coffee. I looked at my watch and agreed, not really sure where this was going to lead.

We drove up to her apartment, a space that radiated her artistic spirit. The moment I stepped inside, I felt a sense of warmth and individuality. The furniture was simple yet stylish, with a mix of vintage and modern pieces. Neutral-colored cushions in earthy tones adorned the cozy seating, and the vibrant throw blanket added a splash of color to the otherwise muted tones. Neatly arranged shelves displayed a large collection of books and handcrafted decor. Framed sketches and abstract paintings, likely her own creations, adorned the walls, giving the space an intimate and personal touch.

At every corner, plants and flowers thrived, bringing life and freshness into the room. A vase of wildflowers graced the center table. A vintage record player sat in the corner as Indrani walked toward it and set a vinyl record in place. It played soft, soulful music, adding to the apartment's charm.

Every detail spoke of creativity and warmth.

I looked at her as she excused herself to prepare coffee. She brought it over. As I took the first sip, I complimented her on it.

As I met Indrani's gaze, I felt a surge of excitement mingled with apprehension. The prospect of breaking free from the monotony of corporate life was undeniably alluring, but it also carried a weight of uncertainty.

"What if we took the leap?" I mused, the idea taking root in my mind, like a seedling yearning to grow.

I couldn't help but notice the subtle shift in the air. The tension between us crackled like electricity, igniting a desire that had remained subdued for too long.

Indrani's laughter, once carefree and light, now carried a hint of something deeper, something more intimate. And as our eyes met in the dimly lit apartment, I felt a rush of emotions that I struggled to contain.

Indrani's gaze softened, her eyes mirroring the vulnerability I felt within.

In that moment, the barriers that had separated us melted away, leaving only raw honesty and unspoken desire in their wake. As the distance between us converged, our lips met in a tender embrace, igniting a fire that burned with a passion that could not be extinguished. The world outside ceased to exist, and we were consumed by the intensity of our shared desire. In the quiet solitude of her apartment, amidst the echo of our whispered confessions, we discovered intimacy.

As the night wore on, we lost ourselves in each other. In the quiet stillness of the early hours, I thought that our journey had begun, with endless possibilities stretching out before us like stars in the night sky. Little did I know that the spark that had been ignited would set ablaze a chapter in our lives, leaving many scorched in its wake.

Weeks passed, and insecurity gripped my heart as expectations grew in Indrani's mind—expectations I wasn't prepared to meet. The weight of commitment felt like an anchor threatening to pull me under, drowning the joy that our connection initially brought.

The realization of the futility of our relationship dawned on both of us. The silent moments between us echoed the unspoken truth—that what we shared was a fleeting passion, not meant to weather the storms of a long-term commitment. Indrani, sensing the inevitable, eventually drifted away. I watched her departure with a heavy heart, not attempting to stop her, as I acknowledged the lack of my right to hold her back.

The echoes of our time together reverberated within the walls that had borne witness to our clandestine romance. The corporate environment that once seemed mundane had become the canvas for a complex narrative of love, lust, and insecurities. The phase of my life, from the innocence of childhood in Netaji Nagar to the complexities of adult relationships, felt surreal and disjointed under the same roof.

The walls that had once enclosed our surreptitious encounter now bore witness to the echoes of a love story that had crumbled under the weight of unmet expectations and insecurities. And I, the insecure seeker of validation, was left to navigate the aftermath of a love that had burned too bright and too fast.

As our paths eventually diverged, and she drifted away, it became apparent that I had become just a chapter in her story that she had now chosen to forget—a footnote in the grand narrative of her ambition. Indrani continued her ascent. Her story was not one of compromise but of unapologetic pursuit—a journey marked by victories and sacrifices, a testament to the complexities of a woman who dared to dream and dream big.

Within two months, I decided to move to a more comfortable abode in East of Kailash. This relocation not only brought me closer to work but also distanced me from the mundane environment of Netaji Nagar. However, the illusion of a stable and routine existence was shattered by unforeseen events. I believed I was leaving Netaji Nagar and its memories behind, convinced that I would never cross paths with Indrani again.

Little did I know that the calm facade I had built for my future was about to be disrupted by a storm of events, leaving me vulnerable and exposed.

Chapter 2

The transition from the simplicity of Netaji Nagar to the ostentation of East of Kailash brought about a perceptible change. Everything in this new locale appeared magnified, viewed through a different lens. The plot sizes, house dimensions, sprawling driveways, luxury cars, and even the stature of the residents seemed imbued with an air of grandiosity.

My move to the barsaati, with its unpretentious single room, attached bathroom, and functional kitchen, was undertaken with tempered expectations. As a solitary individual immersed in a demanding job, my requirements were elemental—a space to retire for the night.

My loneliness played havoc with me, and I began to despise my newfound independence, bereft of any genuine relationships. Colleagues like Abhay and Sunil reveled in holiday escapades, Manoj remained enigmatically occupied, Pratip chose a path of relocation to Chennai, and Indrani, in her own mysterious way, seemed to harbor ill will, metaphorically sticking pins into a voodoo doll that bore a semblance to me.

A wannabe cook aspiring to be a chef from Bihar strived hard to fulfill my culinary needs each night. Yet even the national dish of Bihar, Litti Chokha, emerged bland in his hands. In an attempt to infuse variety, I suggested exotic Bihari dishes like Chana Ghugni or Laung-Latika, only to be met with a confused and quizzical look. The culinary span was confined to the familiar terrain of Rajma-chawal and Aloo-gobi.

Simple pleasures and taken-for-granted conveniences of life—a sumptuous meal, timely medical attention, or even the mundane act of sewing a missing button—had become elusive chores.

Yearning for a change in scenery and a professional makeover, I bid adieu to Altos India, venturing into the glamorous and exciting world of an advertising firm. This was in major contrast to the lackluster and boring environment of an IT firm.

The interview at the advertising agency presented an unexpected challenge—the creation of an advertising slogan for a coal-producing company. The catchphrase "NOT EVERYTHING ABOUT US IS BLACK" found favor, culminating in an offer letter. The nascent days at the new workplace unfolded graciously, as I shared a workspace with Hitesh, an egoistic yet vibrant copywriter.

Hitesh Jain, at 32, embodied a fascinating blend of egoism and vibrancy that set him apart in any room. His ego, often mistaken for arrogance, was more a manifestation of his unshakable confidence in his abilities. He wore it like a badge of honor, seeking validation and recognition for his work with an unapologetic fervor. Yet, beneath this facade lay an undeniable charm, a vibrant energy that lit up any workspace he inhabited.

Hitesh was driven by a deep passion for excellence and a love for overcoming challenges. He approached obstacles as opportunities to grow and showcase his skills. He was unapologetically political, weaving his way through the corridors of power with consummate ease. His creativity was unmatched, weaving stories and narratives that resonated deeply with audiences. It was this unique talent and dedication that elevated him to the top of the advertising world, where his work continued to captivate.

However, Hitesh was not without his flaws. His competitive spirit often bordered on ruthlessness, driving him to go to any lengths to outshine the competition. Collaboration did not come easily to him; his ego often got in the way, making teamwork a challenge. Yet, for those who could see past his bravado, there was no denying his brilliance.

Born and raised in Mumbai, Hitesh's journey to success was anything but easy. Against the odds, he pursued his passion for writing, defying the expectations of his family and society. He cut his teeth in the advertising industry, quickly making a name for himself with his bold ideas and razor-sharp wit.

Love him or hate him, Hitesh Jain was a force to be reckoned with, a relentless powerhouse of creativity and ambition.

An intriguing dynamic unfolded as our professional collaboration flourished, prompting Hitesh to entrust me with more responsibilities.

The turning point came when Hitesh proposed a content research project centered on the socially significant cause of sex trafficking. The project delved into the lives of sex workers in Delhi's notorious G.B. Road, presenting an intriguing avenue for exploration and societal introspection. The socially charged nature of the assignment stirred my curiosity. Little did I realize that this would pave the way for an unconventional collaboration that would bring together the past and weave its way into my future.

"I wanted to discuss the new project that just came in. It's a campaign focused on raising awareness about sex trafficking issues, particularly centered around G.B. Road."

"That's heavy, but I'm glad we're tackling such a crucial issue. What's the scope of the project?"

"It's quite comprehensive. The client wants us to create a multi-platform campaign that educates the public about the realities of sex trafficking, dispels myths, and encourages action and support for victims."

"Got it. We need to make sure our messaging is respectful and doesn't sensationalize the issue."

"Exactly," said Hitesh. "It's crucial that we handle this with the utmost care and empathy."

"How about we start by researching the specific challenges faced by victims in G.B. Road?" I suggested.

"That sounds like a solid plan. We should think about incorporating survivor stories into the campaign. Their voices are powerful and can help humanize the issue for the audience. I think collaborating with organizations that have first-hand experience and expertise will ensure our campaign is well-informed and impactful. Hey, speaking of partnerships, I know someone who could be a great addition to our team for this project. I forget her name, but I do know that she has done some fantastic work in this space before. She runs a company that does a lot of content research and ghostwriting for many well-known and reputed companies and individuals and is also one of the agencies that is pitching for an empanelment with our publishing business line."

"Where do we fit in?" I asked.

"It is fairly straightforward. She provides content, does ghostwriting, and would like to use our machinery to get some solid stuff off the ground. Guess she needs to tide over some speed bumps she has hit along the way and is under tough times and would like to ride on the back of our infrastructure and contacts. I'm sure she could also use the money. This could be a test for her to prove her credentials as well."

"Fantastic. I am confident we can create an even more impactful campaign."

Hitesh agreed. "I'll ask my team to reach out to her and see if she's interested. I have a feeling she'll be just as passionate about this project as we are. Let's get going. I'm sure this will be a powerful campaign."

I nodded.

"Here is the broad snapshot to give you an idea." He handed over a bunch of papers to me. "I think you will be heading out tomorrow morning to start on this. Be here by 7 AM. I will ask my team to schedule your meeting with what's-her-name at the same time."

I picked up the documents from the table and gave them a summary once-over.

"Given the size of the contract, wouldn't you like to be more directly involved?" I asked as I looked at the value of the contract in seven figures.

"This research is one element of the overall contract, dude," Hitesh said. "I will come in later. Besides, I have the other deal with the fashion clothing line and a final meeting with the Communications Director lined up. I need to prepare for that. If Maya likes my pitch, then we are going to move ahead with the contract. Cheers and good luck." He then walked out without even a second glance.

This was typical Hitesh—straight, to the point, and matter-of-fact.

Tomorrow should be an interesting day. It promised to be the commencement of an intriguing exploration into the complexities of life, relationships, and societal issues.

I woke up startled at the sound of the alarm clock. It was 5:30 AM, and I had to get ready for the important assignment. The morning air was crisp as I made my way through the bustling streets, the anticipation of the day's tasks weighing heavily on my mind. The importance of the assignment loomed large, driving me forward with a sense of purpose.

Arriving at the office building, I parked my bike and strode through the entrance, my steps quickening as I neared the reception area, acutely aware that I was late. It was almost 7:30 AM. There, sitting on the couch, was a figure with their back to me. My heart skipped a beat as I wondered if it could be the same girl I was scheduled to meet to assist me with the research.

"Ouch, that's a bad start. Not very professional," I said to myself.

Hurrying past, I made my way up to my office, my mind already buzzing with plans and preparations. As I gathered my belongings, the shrill ring of the phone pierced the air, jolting me from my thoughts.

"Sir, there is somebody here to see you," came the voice of the security guard, his tone urgent.

"Yes, yes, I am coming," I said, a trifle agitated at being made aware of my poor time management skills.

Nodding to myself, I quickly stowed away my things and headed back downstairs, my curiosity piqued.

Descending the staircase, I found the security guard waiting for me, a look of concern etched on his face. "She has been waiting for a while, sir," he informed me.

With a nod of thanks, I proceeded towards the reception area, my footsteps echoing in the empty corridor. As I drew closer, a sense of foreboding washed over me, the gravity of the situation sinking in.

I paused to recover my breath, ready to face whatever awaited me.

The journey had commenced, and I found myself at the precipice of an adventure that would alter the very fabric of my being at an emotional and physical level, without the option of turning back.

Chapter 3

Once I had made my way to the reception, amid all the faces that confronted me, I caught a glimpse of familiar eyes that sparked recognition. There she was, Indrani, the fiercely ambitious woman I had once shared stolen moments with. As our eyes met, the memories of our past connection resurfaced, and the air crackled with a tension that hinted at the possibility of unfinished business.

"Indrani?" I uttered, half-expecting her to deny her identity.

"Dinesh?" she countered, pursing her lower lip as the weight of memories dawned upon her. We found ourselves locked in a prolonged gaze, the silence pregnant with unspoken history.

"Perhaps we can go into one of these huddle rooms," I suggested, attempting to diffuse the palpable awkwardness that hung between us.

"That's a good idea," she agreed, gracefully lifting her overstuffed backpack.

Seated in the relatively confined space of the huddle room, I ordered two coffees—a feeble attempt to dispel the lingering discomfort in the air.

"Listen, Indrani—" I began cautiously.

"If you're wanting to bring up the past and what happened between us, then please don't, Dinesh," she interjected. "It's a thing of the past, and both of us enjoyed it as long as it lasted. I have moved on and have this new venture to work on. It is a firm that I have built over the years and have really given it my all. The firm and its success—it's all that matters to me."

As the office peon entered with two paper cups filled with a frothy concoction resembling coffee, we paused our conversation momentarily to express gratitude. The door closed behind him, leaving us in a bubble of awkward tension.

"I launched this firm three years ago," she continued, her gaze focused on me. "It has done well so far, and we've hired freelancers and sourced content and research for our clients. We now have the horsepower to move to the next level of providing our services to big companies like yours. You could outsource all that research and analytical material to us, and we can get them over the line for you."

Her transition from personal matters to business was swift, and it seemed she had more to share.

"I can see you've done well for yourself, Dinesh, and I'm genuinely happy for you," she expressed with sincerity. "I must confess that some of the best moments of my life were the times I got to spend with you. Some things are not fated to be, and we were both too impulsive to understand or appreciate what we were getting into. Let it go now, as I'm sure you have."

Uncertain of how to react, I simply nodded in agreement.

"I've submitted our proposal for a possible empanelment with your company," she revealed. "Hitesh asked me to meet with you on this one project that he wanted me to execute on a trial basis."

"I am happy for you, and if this is getting awkward for you, I can have someone else assigned to this work. Rest assured, I will not let the past interfere with our professional collaboration. You did nothing wrong, and maybe it was just—"

"Let it go, Dinesh," she interrupted gently. "That's what I thought you would say, and I'm perfectly happy to work on this with you. It might help me more to have you witness what I can do. Friends?" She extended her hand, signaling a truce. I realized she had finished her coffee during the conversation.

"Friends," I responded with a sense of relief evident on my face. "It's great to see you again."

We talked for some more time. Indrani had managed to snag a contact in G.B. Road who was willing to let her into this dark world—for a fee, of course. My being assigned to her was perhaps just what she wanted.

"Let's plan out our approach before we head out to G.B. Road," she said with a whisper of a smile on her lips.

"Why do you actually want to visit G.B. Road? Surely, you could read and research this without having to actually go there," I asked.

"This cannot be done remotely, Dinesh. I am doing a story on sex workers, especially the young sex workers. I have been trying to get this meeting organized for a long, long time and finally have been asked to come and meet one person in a Kotha. This is a big breakthrough, and it has taken me weeks to get this set up."

"Sure," I said. She still held a certain charm that I found attractive and endearing.

"I can only offer you my physical presence because I hardly know anything about the place except that…"

"It's a whorehouse," she said, completing what I wanted to say but could not have brought myself to say in front of her. "Yes, it is only your physical presence that I'm looking for," she said, sending my thoughts to another dimension. She smiled almost as if she read my mind. "C'mon, let us go, you naughty dog. You haven't changed. I will fill you in on the history and details on the way so that you are educated about this place and not identify this place as just a whorehouse."

The history of G.B. Road, as I learned through this educational tour, can be traced back to the Mughal era. It is said that there were a total of five red-light areas, or Kothas, in Delhi at that time. The nightlife of Mughal atrocities and patrons flourished, providing a livelihood for sex workers in these areas. Then came the British Raj, when a British collector consolidated all five Kothas into one area and christened it after himself—Garstin Bastion Road, or simply G.B. Road. The name was officially changed to Swami Shradhanand Marg in 1965.

Indrani held out her iPhone and pointed to the link roads and the direction we were heading. It did seem to me that G.B. Road was very well connected. The New Delhi railway station appeared to be just 10 minutes away. Across the road was the Indian Railways Coach Care Centre, where foreign tourists often clicked pictures of poverty and cows on the streets to take home as "authentic" shots of the Third World. Dena Bank and HDFC Bank were located down the lane and, as Indrani explained, were often used by customers who ran out of money in the pursuit of their carnal desires.

"Tell me more about this story you're doing," I asked, trying to seem interested in her assignment but thoroughly distracted by the amazing perfume she wore.

"Oh, it's about young sex workers. You know, it's more rampant and widespread than we think or know."

"Are you saying that all of G.B. Road is replete with Kothas indulging in the prostitution of young girls? That's illegal, isn't it?" I said, obviously sounding naïve.

Indrani smiled. "All of G.B. Road is not that. Women dalaals, mostly original inhabitants of Bangladesh who subsequently settled in India after their marriage, go scouting for young girls in the impoverished villages of the bordering districts of Bangladesh, such as Satkhira, Jessore, Jhinaidah, Meherpur, Rajshahi, Nawabganj, and Joypurhat."

"And?" I asked, suddenly beginning to get interested in the story.

"A woman dalaal scouts for young girls with certain characteristics. Acting as a ghatak (female matchmaker) as a cover-up, she negotiates with the parents and settles a sham marriage with a male dalaal. Then she informs the male dalaal in India. Pretending to be a legitimate bridegroom, he ties the nuptial knot with the young girl. The so-called bridegroom is able to induce the poor parents to give their young daughter for this fake marriage by paying them Rs 15,000 to Rs 20,000."

"Ouch," I exclaimed.

Indrani continued to recite these grim facts with a clinical detachment that highlighted the nature of her profession. To her, these were mere statistics—a part of a story that needed to be concluded.

"We have arrived," she announced abruptly. "Driver, please stop next to that bearded man standing near the red Maruti."

The car obediently halted beside a man whose face lit up with a welcoming smile as we disembarked.

"Aayeeye, madam," the bearded man exclaimed, waving our car to a stop opposite what appeared to be an endless row of hardware shops. Indrani recognized him and stepped out of the car to exchange greetings. "Hello, Prakash. How are you?" She introduced me as a friend, and I reciprocated with a friendly smile.

"We cannot go into the kothas because we need to take permission, and that is rarely given," said Prakash. "The pimps do not want too much publicity, especially since it ruins their dhanda. But I have managed to have one speak to us. It cost a bit, but he can tell you how this whole racket of prostitution of young girls is conducted and managed. Do not ask him his name."

Indrani nodded, and so did I, not knowing why.

Inside the hardware shop, we encountered a slender, bearded man who appeared slightly uneasy. He exchanged glances with both of us before redirecting his gaze to Prakash. A nod from Prakash seemed to alleviate some of the unidentified bearded man's apprehension.

"Namaste," greeted Indrani.

"Salaam Alaikum," he replied. "Prakash Sahib informed me about what you were looking for. Where do you want me to start?" He led the way deeper into the store, with us trailing behind until we entered a smaller room within the expansive hardware shop.

Indrani scrambled for her writing pad and pen, wasting no time in rattling off her brief, covering virtually everything—from the organizational structure at G.B. Road to the type of clientele, to the popular category of sex workers, and to the larger story of young sex workers.

"There exists a three-tier system at G.B. Road," began our bearded informant, occasionally looking around to ensure that he was not being seen by his brethren, thus risking possible expulsion—or even death. "In the first tier are the malkeens. Initially, when they came into this area as young girls, the malkeens themselves operated as sex workers. Some of them, who had demonstrated sufficient enterprise, were able to save enough money and finally became malkeens. About one in 200 becomes a brothel owner." He paused for a sip of water. "In the second rung are the madams. A madam is one who cannot afford a Kotha but has saved some money. She hires a place and keeps two to three young girls who earn for her along with herself. Eventually, she does not prostitute herself but becomes a manager."

"Which tier do the sex workers belong to?" interrupted Indrani.

"I am coming to that," the bearded man said, appearing a trifle miffed at being stopped in his flow.

Indrani returned to her notes.

"The sex workers comprise the third tier at G.B. Road. Here, as many as 60 percent of the sex workers are young girls. The rest are adults. Eventually, when they can no longer earn their living as sex workers, some of them accept petty jobs as housekeepers in the nearby residential colonies like Dilshad Garden and Anand Vihar, while others work as babysitters or cooks for the working sex workers. And when they are unable to keep even those jobs due to physical inability or old age, most are simply forced to move to the pavements, where they are reduced to rag-picking and begging. Some of these women, however, manage to keep in contact with their families in their native places. Later in life, many of them end up earning their livelihood by acting as procurers of young girls, whom they encourage and trap into prostitution."

"A woman doing this to another woman," I thought. "How could they?" The need to survive at any cost drives people to do anything.

"Dalaals are a significant link in the prostitution business. They help both in transporting young girls and selling them to the Kotha malkeens and call-girls. However, sometimes they also act as pimps, supplying young girls to politicians, officials, and businesspeople."

"How does the prostitution of young girls work so seamlessly?" asked Indrani.

"It is not that easy," responded our bearded friend. "The police extort money from traffickers, sex workers, and Kotha malkeens and are even involved in trafficking. After a young girl is brought into a brothel, the Kotha malkeen calls on the local officer and a constable, requesting them to make a new entry for a newly purchased young girl, for which she pays Rs 10,000 to the police. Some of them even have to first satiate the sexual urges of these local officials."

I winced.

"Sab ki setting hoti hai. The farce follows set stages: a trumped-up case is registered against these young girls, falsely alleging that they were trying to solicit clients in a public place. These girls are then arrested and kept in the lock-up while the police prepare a challan, wherein the young girl's age is entered as 21. This entry is sufficient to manipulate all subsequent court proceedings. After this, these girls are produced before a magistrate and released on bail. The police violate all norms and legal rules and regulations with impunity to help perpetuate prostitution within the Kothas. The Kotha malkeen gets an agreement signed by the newly purchased girl on backdated court stamp paper, stating her willingness to work for the malkeen as a domestic servant. Simultaneously, by a false promissory note, the girl states she has taken a loan of Rs 40,000 from the malkeen. By this process, the young girl enters servitude under the rule of the Kotha malkeen. They convince the magistrate of the genuineness of their relationship with the girl, with the police's assistance, and the remand home is then forced to release the girl into the hands of those pretending to be her relatives."

"Seems to be a land of no return," I exclaimed. There was a pause as the bearded man reached out to a glass of water placed in front of him.

"The young girls are supplied along the Delhi-Uttar Pradesh border to the ever-increasing number of truck drivers. Girls from this slum colony have been sold in Arab countries as well. The preference is for the northeastern area, especially the Nepalese girls. Nepalese girls in G.B. Road Kothas are predominantly from Kathmandu, Birgunj, Biratnagar, and Nepalgunj. The demand for Nepalese girls by the Kotha malkeens is high since they are fair in complexion and clients prefer fair-skinned girls. These girls are sold in different brothels in India for up to Nepali Rs 60,000."

There came a gentle knock on the door, and our bearded companion cautiously peered through the gaps in the wooden boards before opening it. A young girl, no more than seven or eight years old, stood on the threshold.

"Abba, maaji bula rahin hai," she uttered in her childlike voice.

"I am just coming," he replied, turning towards us as the young girl waited. "Now, look at her. She is only seven years old and has already ended up here," he said, a rare emotion of sadness creeping into his voice. "Every time I look at her, I begin to hate myself and what I do even more."

"Is she…" Indrani hesitated.

"Not yet, but she is being readied for the profession," our bearded informant answered, almost anticipating the question. "She is currently under the tutelage of one of the madams. Once she is ready, she will either be sold or put up for the night. The madam will take very good care of her, as she will get a lot of money from the first night."

The conversation was disturbing, and a feeling of revulsion washed over me. I exchanged a glance with Prakash and gripped Indrani's arm, signaling that it was time to go. The little girl continued to look at us.

I could not divert my gaze from the picture of innocence before me. Striking blue eyes, jet-black hair, tall for her age, and a smile that reflected pure innocence. Dressed in a floral pink frock, I noticed her mismatched slippers—a poignant symbol of poverty and helplessness. I turned my gaze away, looking at Indrani with a mix of distress and discomfort.

Prakash glanced at Indrani, asking, "Are you done? Shall we leave?"

"Yes," replied Indrani, seemingly detached as she jotted down her final notes and stowed her diary back into her satchel. I, on the other hand, felt extremely uneasy.

"Is there no way she can be rescued or given a better life?" I asked, hoping against hope.

The bearded man looked at me with terror in his eyes. "Shhh, don't ever say that here," he cautioned, his fear palpable. "She is guarded like a hawk, and you can imagine why. You will be killed for even saying so, and no one will even find your body. Everybody is mixed up in this racket, and there is no way out. I think you should leave before they start sending others to look for me and find you here as well." He looked genuinely worried, urging us to leave.

As we hastily rose from our seats, my gaze continued to be drawn to the small figure standing near the door, a lone sentinel amidst the turmoil. The flickering light cast eerie shadows across her face, accentuating the stark reality of her presence amidst the darkness that enveloped us.

Her presence served as a haunting reminder of the harsh realities that lurked just beyond the threshold of our seemingly ordinary world. In her innocent eyes, I saw a reflection of the innocence that had been shattered by the horrors of G.B. Road—a reminder of the innocence lost amidst the darkness.

Feeling a surge of anguish and helplessness, I reached into my pocket and retrieved a chocolate bar—a feeble attempt to bring a moment of normalcy to the child amidst the chaos. As she eagerly accepted the token of kindness, a fleeting spark of joy illuminated her eyes—a glimmer of hope amidst the despair.

"What's your name?" I asked softly, my voice barely audible above the din of the room.

"Jannat," she replied, her voice tinged with a haunting echo of the innocence that had been stolen from her.

"Very nice name," I said.

Before I could say another word, she disappeared into the shadows, leaving behind a lingering sense of sorrow and despair. I stood there, my eyes scanning the alley for any trace of her—her fluttering dress, a glimpse of her hair, anything—but the darkness offered no clues.

Indrani tugged at my shirt as we hastily made our way toward the door, the weight of the evening's events hanging heavy in the air. As we stepped out into the night, I couldn't shake the feeling that we had only scratched the surface of the darkness that lurked within the walls of G.B. Road.

After that evening, Indrani remained silent about the harrowing experience.

The research continued for another week, and I accompanied her on each trip. During one such visit, Prakash introduced her to another sex worker. Prakash was clearly getting richer with each introduction he facilitated. The interview moved me and set me on a course that would later change my life.

"Thank you for talking to us. Sorry we are having to talk to you here in the midst of all..." Indrani bit her tongue, but the girl before her only smiled.

"You will perhaps never invite me to visit your family," she said with a resigned tone. "For I am one of the 4,500 sex workers who live and work at G.B. Road, the city's red-light area. No pity, please. I have no objection to selling my body for the sake of roti. Besides, I have become used to this neighborhood. My three boys were born here. The best friendships of my life were made here. My six co-workers live together like sisters. This Kotha is my home.

While we entertain customers throughout the day, evenings are busier. We dress up, apply powder, body lotion, and lipstick, and stand out on the balcony. By then, the thoroughfare has started teeming with cars, scooters, rickshaws, and pull-carts. Men stare up at us while the women, passing by in rickshaws, throw discreet glances. Sometimes, when we spot photographers, we take out our sandals and threaten them.

Our daily customers have gone down from 15 to 2. That we are growing old is not the only reason. A few dalaals, on the payroll of wealthier kothas, solicit customers in front of our stairs. Occasionally, they snatch the mobile phones and wallets of our regulars. When we ask these goons to go away, they dare us to complain to the police.

Nowadays, we are able to get a respectable number of customers only on select occasions—like Republic Day, Independence Day, or during political rallies, when men come visiting the city for a day or two. However, it is the immediate future that appears more worrisome. The government is bringing in a law that will classify our clients as criminals. Who would then come to us? How would we earn? What would become of our children?"

"There's an MCD school here, but I send my boys to the one at Minto Park. G.B. Road is a dangerous place, and I do not want them to keep the wrong company while away from my eyes. Teachers are sympathetic and understand our problems. They have promised not to disclose our address to anyone. You see, my boys are always worried about their friends discovering where they live. Babu, my oldest, wants to be a maulana, and Chhotu a lawyer. I try to bring them up well. A tuition expert comes in the evening to teach them Maths and English. The rest is up to their kismet.

Money is always a problem, but it becomes difficult to sustain your income as you grow older. Some women manage to save and start a new life outside G.B. Road, but I will have to stay on."

"Why..." Indrani started but was interrupted by a loud shout from across the hall, and the girl got up with a start. As the sound of footsteps drew closer, she indicated that we should leave. We got up and left without either of us saying a word, leaving Prakash to handle the aggressive questions posed by the pimp who had brought a customer for the girl we had just spoken to.

A month later, Indrani filed her research document to great appreciation. It was lauded in the media, and Hitesh was over the moon with the outcome. For her, this was just another story—another piece of statistic.

I wondered if the city of Delhi had contributed to that. It numbs you to your sensitivities and robs you of your emotions with each passing day. The stark realities, such as the one we had experienced, only added to the pace of the desensitizing process. The tale unfolded in layers, exposing the intricate dance between survival, dreams, and the harshness of reality on G.B. Road. The delicate balance of hope and despair in the

Kotha, and the relentless passage of time etching its mark on these lives.

As time progressed, my involvement with both my work and Indrani deepened. We resumed seeing each other regularly, and despite my occasional resentment toward her emotionally detached approach to life, I found those very qualities endearing—as necessary survival tools in the city. Recollections of our shared times frequently crossed my mind, prompting me to wonder why our relationship had not evolved further.

Over time, I began growing more attached to her, drawn to facets of her personality previously unseen. Her independence and the ease with which she disconnected and reconnected fascinated me. Each intimate encounter deepened our connection, forging an unspoken bond.

Hitesh, now part of the senior management team, seemed aware of our evolving relationship. His knowing smiles when I sat near his workstation raised questions about his own journey to the top.

One day, he confronted me abruptly, asking, "Are you screwing her?"

"What? Who?" I asked, not knowing how to react.

"Oh, c'mon, dude. Indrani—who else?"

Taken aback, I questioned his intent. He elaborated, highlighting Indrani's influential connections in the industry and the potential benefits of aligning with her. His perspective on relationships and success echoed the city's pragmatic ethos.

A revelation unfolded as Hitesh disclosed that, based on my positive recommendation, the company had formalized a lucrative retainership agreement with Indrani's firm. She had leveraged this success to secure additional clients, using these references to further enhance her reputation. It dawned on me that I might have been more of a means than an end in our interactions.

As I pondered the situation, Hitesh remarked with a smirk, "Well, if you were not screwing her, she definitely screwed you, buddy." Thoughts raced through my mind, connecting the dots of Indrani's behavior—the abrupt departures, unanswered calls, and overall detachment after sealing the significant deal.

The realization hit me: I was the unwitting player in a scheme of payback. She was never truly invested in me emotionally. Our intimate encounter at her apartment had occurred against a backdrop of distractions and her constant texting. She had never truly been in the moment. I wondered if she was as devious as circumstances had revealed.

I had recommended her firm based on the research work she had submitted, not because of the physical intimacy we had once shared. I had probably failed to see that my emotional connection did not necessarily need a reciprocal anchor from her. She had likely played along, and it had worked.

As I gathered my belongings and closed my laptop, the echoes of a lost love reverberated through my mind, interwoven with a profound sense of betrayal. My attempt to reach Indrani proved futile, leaving me with an unsettling feeling of finality in our strained relationship. Despite the emotional turmoil, I found solace in retaining her number—a keepsake that personified the bittersweet memories of what once was.

Navigating the office cubicles, I approached the now-deserted cabin of Hitesh, the architect of my recent revelations. The emptiness within mirrored the void that had formed within me—an unsettling awareness of the complexities entwined in professional and personal relationships.

I made my way toward the parking lot, the weight of the day's events still pressing on my shoulders.

If only I had departed an hour earlier, I might have witnessed the clandestine departure of Hitesh and Mahira, his boss—their actions casting light on the shadowy realm where personal ambitions intersected with professional pursuits.

The city, relentless in its demands, had once again revealed its capacity to shape destinies and alter the course of relationships. As I rode through the bustling streets, I could not help but reflect on the bizarre dance of power, ambition, and the unseen forces that orchestrated the heady concoction of success and survival in the urban jungle.

Chapter 4

Maya's association with a reputed clothing line had seamlessly intertwined with Hitesh's professional endeavors, adding a layer of mystery to their connection. While Hitesh embodied a carefree spirit, Maya exuded a refined aura, sparking curiosity about the dynamics of their relationship.

I couldn't help but attach similarities to the relationship that Indrani and I had shared with what Hitesh and Maya were seemingly heading towards or so I thought. The pattern seemed familiar but I had been colored and scarred by my experiences and had perhaps lost the ability to distinguish between platonic relationships and other associations nurtured with an intention to accomplish insidious intentions.

Maya, the Communications Director with a reputed clothing line and Hitesh had her account to manage. Due to the high value of the contract, Hitesh was required to personally oversee the account. A series of new style launches necessitated Maya's interaction with Hitesh and vice versa on very frequent basis.

Maya, with her dark ebony skin, was born and brought up in Assam. She decided to leave her home state to chase her dreams in Mumbai, eventually moving to Delhi to lead the communications team. Her personality showed strength and resilience, but she carried a shadow of insecurity wherever she went.

Her insecurity stemmed from many things, her difficult childhood, a broken marriage, and the harsh comments she often heard about her skin color. Growing up in such an environment made her self-doubt a deep part of who she was, a part she truly despised. This insecurity showed itself in small but clear ways. She spoke with hesitation during team meetings, as though she doubted her own voice. At times, she would steal quick glances in the mirror, studying her reflection, trying to find something to feel confident about.

Hitesh, found himself unwittingly drawn into the complexities of Maya's journey.. The corporate world, with its unspoken standards of beauty, had planted seeds of self-doubt in Maya's mind, leaving her yearning for validation that seemed elusive.

One day, as the pressures of work and the weight of her insecurities converged, Maya found herself seeking solace in the quiet corners of the office. Hitesh, unsuspecting, became an unwitting confidant. Late-night conversations evolved from work-related discussions to Maya's vulnerabilities, and Hitesh found himself navigating the delicate terrain of her self-esteem.

"Let's not talk about it Hitesh. It upsets me all the time."

"Perhaps I can help Maya. If you push away people who want to help you or listen to you then you are going to further go down a dark hole. I really want to listen to you. Consider me a friend."

"I have really tried to put all my negativity behind me Hitesh, but some things keep coming back to me. My relatively poor upbringing in Assam, being married to an abusive man who I finally managed to divorce and now this constant reminder that I am dark complexioned. Is that we are all truly about?"

Hitesh could understand where she was coming from and instinctively hugged her. She cried on his shoulders for a very long time and Hitesh did not want to pull away.

There were moments marked by fragility and an overwhelming desire to feel desired, to find reassurance in the arms of someone who seemed to offer an escape from the harsh judgments that plagued her.

Hitesh, caught in the throes of Maya's vulnerability had reciprocated with a mixture of compassion and confusion. The intimate encounters became a fleeting respite for Maya, a momentary distraction from the harsh realities she faced daily.

"Great results for the quarter and its time to party." yelled Hitesh from the other end of the office. "We have got the contract with Alps Clothing." The invitation to Hitesh's soiree, echoed through the halls of the company.

"Is it just for the team here?" I asked.

"Bring your friend along," he suggested, weaving the promise of an eclectic gathering where connections would blossom amid the revelry. Yet, I found myself caught in the conundrum of identifying a suitable companion for the evening.

Hitesh, nonchalant and reassuring, dismissed my concerns with a cryptic assurance. "Don't worry if you do not have one. There will be enough to choose from at my party."

The entrance into the nightclub hosting the festivities marked the zone which was truly Hitesh's playground. Alcohol flowed freely, and the pulsating rhythm of music filled the air, setting the backdrop for the interplay of diverse personalities.

Maya's presence added a new dimension to the already vibrant mix of characters. Her origins in Assam lent her an aura of mystery, her background shrouded in the misty hills and lush greenery of the region.

With a figure sculpted through hours of Pilates and crunches, Maya carried herself with an effortless elegance that spoke of discipline and dedication. Her sleek silhouette and flawless posture were a testament to her commitment to both physical fitness and self-care. She had decided to fight and that was evident in her every step.

But it wasn't just Maya's appearance that set her apart—it was the enigmatic energy that seemed to surround her like a veil. There was a depth to her gaze, a hint of secrets hidden behind those mesmerizing eyes. She spoke with the lilt of her native Assamese tongue, adding to her allure. Whether she was engaged in conversation or lost in thought, there was always an air of mystery about her, As the evening wore on, it became clear that Maya was not just a character in the story—but the very heart and soul of it.

"Thank you Maya for the contract. I promise that our firm will workday and night to make your clothing line and you are super successful."

"I have no doubt you will, Hitesh."

The blurry intent was getting clearer as the night wore on and I watched as the nefarious designs began unfolding right in front of my eyes.

It was evident to me that Maya was harboring aspirations to ensnare Hitesh as a prize catch. My observations hinted at eddies beneath the surface. As the night progressed, it became evident that Maya's apparent sobriety was a facade. She accepted drinks graciously but, refrained from consuming them, tipping the glass into the foliage when nobody was looking. A sense of curiosity gnawed at me as I pondered the reasons behind her unconventional behavior.

"Just why was she doing that?" I wondered.

Maya's gaze remained fixed on Hitesh throughout the night, an unspoken connection resonating between them. On multiple occasions, she extended a helping hand to a progressively inebriated Hitesh, maintaining a composed demeanor despite the revelry around them. Something was going on, but it was hard for me to figure out what it really was.

As the clock struck two and the party began winding down, Maya assumed a role beyond the vivacious partygoer. She approached Hitesh with a blend of concern and authority, signaling that it was time to depart. The restaurant was clearing out, and an air of sobriety crept in. Hitesh, reliant on her for support, seemed to agree with her suggestion.

"It is time to go Hitesh." I heard her say to him "I have had too much to drink and so have you."

"Really?" I thought.

He leaned over and clung onto her shoulders for support. The restaurant was beginning to close and almost all the guests had departed. "Let me drop you back home and you can collect your car from here tomorrow."

Hitesh seemed to agree but was clearly too sozzled to say anything otherwise.

" It may not be too safe at this time of the night just in case there is trouble on the way." I said. offering my assistance to drop them home. I only had a couple of glasses of wine and clearly capable of passing any test along the way. Maya was sober so she was qualified too but I was unsure how this was all playing along.

Maya, however, dismissed my offer with unexpected annoyance, asserting that she could manage. I acquiesced, albeit with a lingering sense of uncertainty. "It's fine," she said, "I can manage."

I ignored the aggression in her tone. "No, I insist. Just wait for me. I need to take a quick leak and will be right back."

Upon returning, the valet confirmed that Maya and a `drunk man' had left without waiting for me. I decided to follow them.

Something was bothering me in my head. I drove with caution in the direction of Hitesh's house, looking around for a BMW as I drove but there was no sign of either the car, Hitesh or Maya.

Soon, I had reached Hitesh's apartment complex. I beckoned to the guard who walked gingerly towards me.

"Is Hitesh saab here?" I inquired, and the guard responded with a smile, noting that a woman had driven the car and had just brought Hitesh saab back home. Relief washed over me, thinking, "At least Hitesh has reached home safely."

"Do you want to go in too?" the guard asked.

"No, I don't think so. He must be tired and probably fast asleep by now," I replied.

"I don't think so, saab. The lady who came to drop him has not left and is still there in his apartment,".

Six months elapsed, marking the passage of time since Hitesh and Maya's subdued wedding ceremony. The once-celebratory ambiance of the party where their connection had first blossomed now stood in stark contrast to the palpable frostiness evident in their relationship. The intimacy was clearly missing and that added layers of confusion and complexity hinting at a fractured union.

The office was quiet as Hitesh and I found ourselves alone in the breakroom, surrounded by the hum of vending machines and the distant clatter of keyboards. It was a moment I had been avoiding, but curiosity and a desire for clarity compelled me to broach the subject that had lingered in the background of our relationship. In a rare moment of candor, I mustered the courage to confront Hitesh about the intricacies of their relationship.

"Hitesh, there's something I've been meaning to ask you. It's a personal question so I apologize if I am intruding."

Hitesh, looking up from his coffee, met my gaze with a mixture of curiosity and apprehension.

"Sure, go ahead. What's on your mind?"

"Why did you marry Maya? I mean, considering everything—the complexities, the ups and downs. What made you choose her? It was all so sudden. None of my business but I had to ask you as it took us all by surprise."

Hitesh's expression shifted, a combination of contemplation and a hint of vulnerability.

"That's bloody random." He said. "It's not a simple answer, really. Maya and I, we met during a time when we both needed support. There was a genuine connection, and I believed that love could conquer the challenges we faced. Maya was going through a difficult phase, and I suppose I provided a sense of stability and understanding. I genuinely cared for her, and I thought our connection could lead to a stronger relationship.

"And now?"

Hitesh sighed, his eyes carrying the weight of unspoken truths.

"Over time…complexities emerged, and it became clear that our reasons for being together were more about filling voids than building a solid partnership."

"Do you regret marrying her?"

Hitesh paused to answer "No, I don't regret it but…"

There was enough said in those unsaid words.

Hitesh soon resigned from the company and transitioned to another reputable advertising firm. His ability to land plum jobs left me jealous, leaving me intrigued about the key to his professional success.

We were meeting over drinks and it turned into an impromptu task delegation session. I needed a large suitcase and I did not know of who else to contact but Hitesh. Definitely not Indrani.

His fascination with innovative technology was evident, and the coveted iPhone16 he requested for, was now on my shopping list. I had no intention of picking one for myself so this request seemed ok to me. In any case, he was paying for his stuff.

I noticed him looking at his watch impatiently. I reckoned that was his very polite way of asking me to get lost.

"Ok buddy. I will take your leave." I said as I got up to leave on cue.

He smiled and said a quick goodbye with his mobile cradled on his shoulder as he answered the phone following the chime of a received message. He walked into the other room and I thought I heard the name Mahira or was it Maya. Maybe I wasn't hearing right. I was progressively getting confused. I was wondering why there was no mention of Maya that evening. "Was she still part of his life or were new chapters being written."

I let the thought pass. The city had taught me to never think straight.

My Florida trip unfolded with a mix of official duties and personal indulgences. The bustling atmosphere of international travel enveloped me as I acquired not only the 'iPhone16' but also an Apple iWatch and a Mac. Stepping into the swagger of a typical Delhiite, I nonchalantly pushed my trolley through customs, witnessing a Sikh gentleman maneuvering an oversized trolley laden with electronic treasures with a nod of familiarity exchanged with the customs official.

"I would probably get to see those items at Ghaffar Market tomorrow," I thought as I moved towards the driver who had the placard with my name on it. He grabbed the trolley almost as if I had brought things for his family.

Back in Delhi, a week later, the urgency to hand over the iPhone16 to Hitesh took precedence. Multiple attempts to contact him yielded no response, forcing me to seek the assistance of an office boy. As I carefully packed the box, I included a note specifying the owed amount, ensuring it reached Hitesh's hands only.

"I know Hitesh saab. I will hand it over to him or his wife," The office boy reassured.

"Good," I said. Make sure you collect the payment. Here is the address."

The office boy returned in the evening and I confirmed with him whether he had handed it over to Hitesh.

"You gave me the wrong address sirjee. Luckily, I met the neighbor who was his friend and he gave me his current address. I then had to take an auto and it cost me..."

"I am not interested in all the details. I will reimburse you for that, do not worry. What did he say, and did he give you the money? He did not even call me."

"Hitesh saab was not there at home, so I handed the packet to his wife. She said that she would let Hitesh know and call you to thank you. She gave me the money and even gave me Rs. 100 as a tip," said the office boy, clearly delighted by his experience.

"That is great. I hope you gave it to the right address and the right person," I asked again.

"Yes, sir. The address was right as it had his name on the nameplate. The lady said she was his wife and that she would hand it over to him. A genuinely nice woman."

"Maya is her name," I said as I took the money from him.

"Oh, okay. All that I know is that she is tall and gori. I have even taken a receiving note from her," the office boy continued, now appearing somewhat worried at the prospect of having given the packet to someone else.

The triumphant office boy had returned with the assurance that Hitesh would call to chat with Dinesh later. The narrative, however, took an unexpected turn when he described the woman as tall and fair—a stark contrast to Hitesh's previous descriptions of Maya.

"Tall and gori?" I repeated. That did not sound like Maya. I thought, *Maya was dark, and that was something Hitesh always held against her.* "Then who was this?"

"Show me the receiving note," I said to the office boy, betraying my impatience.Scrawled across the piece of paper that was handed over to me by the office boy were the words 'Received packet with thanks. Signed with a flourish underneath was the name 'Mahira.'

Hitesh would not be calling me.

The interactions died post that day and it was not long before a common friend sent me an update post on Facebook.

Hitesh and Maya had left the city to start a new life in Singapore. A candid photo showed them walking hand in hand, the Marina Bay Sands gleaming in the background. Their smiles were as bright as the skyline, and their captions spoke of hope and fresh starts.

Chapter 5

Several years had passed before I decided to bid farewell to my humble barsaati in East of Kailash and relocate to Malviya Nagar, often dubbed as the abode of refugees. It was a transition that added a unique flavor to my life, having previously experienced the spacious government Type 4 houses in Netaji Nagar and the upscale ambience of East of Kailash. Now, I found myself navigating the labyrinthine lanes of a refugee colony, a term that seemed increasingly fitting with each passing day.

Malviya Nagar presented a stark contrast to my previous residences. The houses were crammed together, each resembling an architectural puzzle. Plots as small as 60 square yards boasted three or four-bedroom houses arranged in a peculiar assembly line—living room, bedroom, another bedroom, and finally, the toilet. Space was at a premium, and I quickly realized that this would be a unique and challenging experience.

My decision to move to Malviya Nagar was due to a combination of factors. Firstly, it offered a larger living space compared to the barsaati that had been my home for nearly two years. Secondly, and perhaps more significantly, it was a more budget-friendly option. The less glamorous the area, the lower the rent. Lastly, there was the undeniable allure of being in South Delhi—a crucial factor for social acceptance. In Delhi, belonging to the well-heeled crowd of South Delhi, or at least some parts of it, carried its own significance.

Upon meeting my prospective Bihari landlord, the customary question of "Kaam kahaan karte ho?" was posed.

"Software company hai," I replied.

The follow-up query, "Indian?" hinted at lingering colonial instincts.

"Nahin, American," I replied.

His eyes lit up. It is amazing to notice that we still retain our colonial instincts despite all these years. If nothing else, I knew I had one thing that would work to my great advantage: my roots—my ultimate trump card in dealing with professional landlords.

"Rehne waale kahaan ke ho?" he continued.

"Kerala," I replied.

His eyes lit up like bright torches in a dark sky. However, my trump card was my roots. Hailing from Kerala had a positive impact, enhancing my acceptability. A Keralite boy—or rather a "Malayalam" boy, as most Delhiites refer to Malayalees—working in a good firm is what most "professional" landlords aspire to have either for their daughters or for their house. In both cases, it ensures the property will be well looked after.

"Kerala mein kahaan?" (Where in Kerala?) my prospective landlord inquired. This is such a common question. It's almost as if all of India is your fiefdom, and you would invariably establish a connecting link if I were to tell you where.

"Palakkad," I replied.

"Oh, such a beautiful place. I had gone there on a holiday many years ago and would love to go there again."

I could see that he was beginning to enjoy the conversation, and I began to look around.

As negotiations unfolded, the landlord's excitement grew upon learning about my Kerala origins. The deal was sealed, and I was set to move in by March 1st, albeit after a brief uncertainty caused by the landlord's initial commitment to another tenant. The rent settled at Rs. 2,750 per month, with a deposit of three months' rent. The house, a quintessential representation of "old refugee money finding a new modern environment," featured mismatched furniture and an eclectic mix of items on display: plastic flowers adorning over a million deities, flickering bulbs outlining a particular section of the cabinet around the area where the statues and pictures of the gods and goddesses were placed, old VHS tapes of Ramayana and Mahabharat along with the James Bond collection, and so on.

From the corner of my eye, I thought I sensed the curtain move a wee bit and a pair of eyes trying to squeeze a view from within the many folds, but I ignored it.

"There is a problem," the landlord said again. "I have actually already committed to give this house to another person."

"Then why did I have to be subjected to the interrogation?" I thought to myself.

"I will need to check with him, and if he is not interested, then I can consider you," he said as he turned to spit out the paan he was chewing into the ashtray that had already assumed a color different from its initial hue.

I thanked him and left, a trifle annoyed that he had taken so much time to ask me about my antecedents while fully aware he had already spoken to another and made a commitment. It was well past 7 p.m., and as I was about to straddle my Kawasaki

Bajaj to take me back to my barsaati at East of Kailash, I thought I heard somebody call out my name.

I looked up, and it was the landlord gesturing that I come back. "Possible change of heart," I thought, not knowing what to expect.

I steadied my bike and went up the stairs for the second time. This time, the room was populated with more people than I thought were present earlier. Two girls who looked like they were in their early teens and an elderly lady, presumably the landlord's wife, now occupied the space.

"I have spoken to the other guy and told him that I was keen to give the house to you," the landlord said. "You are a nice boy. You can come in by the 1st of March, and the rent will be Rs. 3,000 per month plus electricity and other charges as per actuals."

I was elated, though uncertain about a man who opened and closed deals so swiftly. "Can we look at Rs. 2,500 as the rent since I have just started work?"

He looked at his wife and daughters. I thought I saw one of the daughters give a slight shake, indicating agreement.

"Okay, Rs. 2,750 per month with a revision in six months' time. You will also have to give a deposit of three months' rent as security, which will be refunded to you at the time of vacation. This will be an interest-free deposit," he said with a wry smile.

I thought of negotiating it down to two months' deposit but decided against it. I did not want him to change his mind again. Having already sampled his decision-making capabilities, I did not want another taste of it. I agreed and left the place, relieved to have resolved a long-vexing issue.

As I straddled my bike for the second time that evening, I instinctively looked up to get an idea of the facade. I could not see much in the dark. As I revved up my bike, shifted to first gear, and moved, I thought I saw the elder daughter wave to me from the corner of my eye. "Had I just imagined it? I wasn't sure." It had been an exceptionally long night, after all.

On the bustling moving day, a rickety tempo traveler trundled into the narrow lane of Malviya Nagar, bearing my austere possessions. The sun beat down relentlessly, casting harsh shadows on the worn-out carpet bundled atop the bed box. The laborers, a motley crew mostly hailing from Bihar, spilled out of the vehicle with an air of determined efficiency, each one assuming their designated role in the chaotic ballet of relocation.

With synchronized movements honed through countless moves, they hoisted the bed box onto their shoulders, navigated the unwieldy TV set through the narrow doorway, and wrestled with the stubborn legs of the table and chair. Amidst the cacophony of grunts and shouted instructions, a momentary lapse in judgment resulted in an unintentional display of "Playboy" centerfolds fluttering to the ground as the doors of the bed box swung open—much to the embarrassment of all involved.

From the vantage point of the first-floor balcony, the landlord observed the spectacle with a mixture of amusement and concern.

"Is that all you have?" he queried. Thankfully, he had missed the "Playboy" centerfold episode.

"Yes, Uncle, that's all. I would have bought more things, but I have to pay rent too," I said sarcastically and laughed at my own attempt at humor. He did not smile.

I returned indoors to arrange my belongings properly. It shouldn't have taken so much time, but I enjoyed seeing everything in its proper place.

As I finished meticulously arranging every piece of furniture in my new apartment, a sense of accomplishment washed over me. The bed was perfectly positioned against the wall, the cupboard stood tall and sturdy in the corner, and the TV set was adjusted just right for optimal viewing.

The unexpected chime of the doorbell shattered the peaceful atmosphere I had created.

I hesitated, momentarily contemplating whether to answer the door or continue reveling in the satisfaction of my newly arranged space. However, with a sigh, I made my way to the door, my footsteps echoing in the empty hallway.

With a few awkward fumbles with the unfamiliar latch, I finally managed to swing the door open. Standing on the other side was the landlord's daughter, a figure I vaguely remembered glimpsing as I had left the house earlier that day. She stood there holding a metal tray adorned with a steaming cup of tea and a plate of biscuits, a hesitant smile playing on her lips.

"Mom has sent this," she spoke softly, her voice barely above a whisper, indicating that her mother had sent the refreshments.

I accepted the tray with a grateful nod, feeling a wave of warmth wash over me at the unexpected gesture of hospitality. As she handed it over, our eyes briefly met, and for a fleeting moment, I detected a shy glimmer of recognition in her gaze.

"Thank you," I murmured sincerely, a genuine smile spreading across my lips.

Her own smile widened in response, and with a quick nod, she turned on her heel and darted back down the stairs, leaving me standing there, more puzzled than ever before.

As I closed the door behind me, the scent of freshly brewed tea filled the air, mingling with the faint aroma of the biscuits. Settling into the coziness of my new home,

I couldn't help but wonder about the landlord's daughter and the mysteries that seemed to surround her shy yet thoughtful gesture.

Malviya Nagar became the backdrop of various life events. Trips to the local market to buy the essentials—bread, butter, and eggs—became part of the routine, where encounters with the golgappa vendor showcased the peculiarities of daily life.

As I walked to the market, honking cars instinctively made me move aside. The chaotic symphony of the market continued, uncaring as usual. Parents guided their children through the bustling marketplace.

Bread and eggs procured, I passed by a meat shop where the daily supply of chicken had just arrived. Over fifty grilled containers, each stacked one on top of another, contained live chickens barely able to breathe. The ordeal of travel seemed overwhelming, yet these chickens somehow survived, albeit some perishing en route. "All dead chicken looks the same anyway," I reasoned.

As I went about my daily routines, the idea of moving to the adjoining colony of Khirki Extension occasionally crossed my mind. Its only allure was its promise of really low rentals and perhaps a chance at a more affordable lifestyle. Despite the allure, I couldn't bring myself to take a resolute step in that direction. I hesitated, unwilling to risk my safety and security for the sake of a few rupees saved on rent. The thought of leaving behind the familiar comforts of my current neighborhood filled me with a sense of dread, as if by venturing into Khirki Extension, I would be stepping into the very heart of darkness itself.

I continued to navigate the twists and turns of city life, juggling the mundane and the extraordinary. In a city as vast and unpredictable as Delhi, sometimes the greatest dangers lie hidden in plain sight, waiting to ensnare the unwary in their sinister embrace.

Little did I know, the essence of Khirki Village would come back to haunt me in the near future, but this time, it would be in the form of a painful encounter, leaving me reeling under its impact for years to come.

Chapter 6

The mobile ringtone buzzed as I rushed over to pick it up. It said "Sunil" calling, and I quickly pressed the accept button.

"Have you found a place yet?" said Sunil, coming straight to the point. He had just returned from work and was helping me find a good house to buy in Saket.

"Not yet, but I do have a broker showing me a house today in Saket," I said almost immediately.

Saket brought back instant memories. The place, which had its first multiplex by the name of Anupam PVR, rarely screened good films in its earlier days—old, worn-out trash. But once it transformed into a multiplex, people thronged in droves. Over time, the place became a focal point around which pubs, restaurants, and more spaces opened up.

"Ok, good. Let me know if you need any help," he said and cut the call.

Barely had I put the phone down when it rang yet again. This time it was the broker.

"Hello, Sir," he exclaimed in his smarmy tone. "The house is ready. It is a good deal, and I think it will be perfect for you."

"What kind of accommodation is it?"

"DDA ka hai, Sir, but why don't you have a look at it?"

As I hurried through my morning routine, I couldn't shake off the nagging sense of anticipation. I climbed into my car and navigated the familiar streets of Delhi, each turn bringing me closer to my destination—the Anupam multiplex.

I had arrived well before the appointed time, with the early morning sun casting long shadows across the deserted parking lot. As I waited for the broker to arrive, my eyes wandered idly over the colorful array of movie posters that adorned the walls of the multiplex. And then, amidst the sea of familiar faces and blockbuster titles, my gaze came to rest on a poster that sent a shiver down my spine. It was the Emraan Hashmi starrer film, Jannat.

There was something about that poster, something elusive yet strangely familiar, that stirred a dormant memory within me. I couldn't put a finger on it. As I stood there, lost in my thoughts, a single question echoed through the recesses of my mind, its answer tantalizingly out of reach. "Wasn't that...?"

"Hello, Sir, are you Dinesh?"

"Yes, I am," I said, not minding the interruption to my chain of thought.

"Sorry I am a little late. Ready to go?" The broker grinned from ear to ear.

"Sure," I said, following him through one of the alleys behind the Anupam complex. I let my thoughts wander.

"We can walk. It's faster that way," he said, leading the way.

Soon, we stood in front of a building that had strayed far from its original design. It sprawled in all directions, completely ignoring approved floor plans. Each floor had its own quirky style, an odd mix of character and over-the-top opulence.

As I stood in the worn-out DDA flat, I couldn't help but feel a mix of amusement and disbelief at the creative ideas the broker was throwing at me. It felt like a crash course in the balance between bending rules and finding convenience.

Climbing the stairs to the first floor, I felt a slight unease creeping in. The broker, clearly experienced, wrestled with the stubborn lock. The metallic clatter echoed through the stale air before the door creaked open, grudgingly.

Crossing the threshold, my heart sank a little. Dust blanketed everything, with stray beams of sunlight streaming through grimy windows. Cobwebs clung to every corner, like evidence of years of neglect.

The walls, once symbols of security, now bore the weight of time. Cracks were visible across the plaster. In one corner, a water-stained patch had turned the wall into a rusty mess, a clear sign of long-term decay.

I hesitated, my steps slowing as I took in the sorry state of the place. "Was this really the home I had come to see? Was this crumbling shell the future I'd imagined?"

A part of me refused to give in to doubt. "What the hell," I thought. I was already here; I might as well make the most of it.

With a bit of resolve, I walked further into the gloom, determined to see if there was any potential hidden beneath the neglect.

"Two bedrooms with attached bathrooms, Sir, and one study," the broker said, gesturing like a salesman unveiling a prize.

I raised an eyebrow at his bold idea of converting the open balcony into a study.

"Good work, isn't it?" he asked with a confident grin, as if expecting instant approval.

I nodded, not out of genuine agreement, but more as an acknowledgment of the sheer audacity of such ideas. As the broker kept sharing stories about unauthorized extensions and creative arrangements with neighbors, I felt like I was being initiated into a hidden society of Delhi's real estate renegades. Each story painted a sordid picture where rules were bent, boundaries blurred, and the line between legality and opportunism rendered optional.

"So, what do you think? A little imagination, a touch of renovation, and voilà! You've got yourself a cozy study overlooking the bustling streets of Delhi," he said with a flourish.

I raised an eyebrow. "Turning the balcony into a study, huh? It's certainly … creative."

I had seen enough. As we left the apartment and descended the stairs, I couldn't help but glance at the maze of unauthorized structures. Each one seemed to tell a story of someone's quest for a little more space, a little more comfort, and maybe a little freedom from the constraints of city living.

Turning a first-floor extension into a ground-floor ceiling? It felt like something out of a heist movie—a daring mix of engineering and rule-bending that blurred the line between necessity and audacity.

Yet, as I listened to the broker's tales with equal parts fascination and disbelief, I found myself admiring the ingenuity of those who navigated this murky world. In a city where space was scarce and opportunities hid in every corner, it seemed to take a special kind of boldness to carve out a niche.

"And there's a garage too, with a servant quarter on top," he added, as though revealing an unexpected bonus. My mind started processing—potential rental income, additional living space…

The stench from the bathroom and the fluttering pigeons made the place feel abandoned, yet the broker remained unfazed. He pointed out the property's potential with the enthusiasm of a salesman showcasing a hidden gem.

As I considered the possibilities, his tone shifted slightly. There was a rare moment of caution in his voice. The garage and servant quarter, it turned out, had sometimes been used for less-than-legitimate purposes. An unspoken truth lingered: when bending rules, you might end up tangled in a web of questionable associations.

However, beyond the real estate deal that was unfolding its many layers, there was a coincidence that had gone unnoticed. The person who had lost her meaning and the place that had lost its relevance with the passage of time had reappeared, reminding me of what I had sworn never to forget. The moment, however fleeting, would return for sure, but I was uncertain if there would still be time to execute a plan I had contemplated in the spur of that heart-rending moment.

"Had I missed the opportunity?" I found myself asking that question.

I didn't have an answer—or, admittedly, didn't want to.

Chapter 7

There was an understated elegance about the way she moved—or was it just the way she had draped the saree around her? There is an allure to a woman who wears a saree, and I was instantly attracted to her. This was a different feeling, unlike anything I had experienced before.

Here I was, in the officious grandeur of a diplomatic mission party, where known bureaucrats and celebrities jostled with one another to the muted beats of exotic music. After exchanging a few pleasantries, I found myself staring at the one figure who seemed supremely disinterested in everything around her, almost as if this was a task to complete rather than an evening to enjoy. Little did I anticipate that this night would become the overture to a love story—unplanned, unscripted, and deeply serendipitous.

As she walked towards the bar without engaging much with anyone around her, I could sense that she was supremely bored and just wanted the evening to end. Her glance met mine and stayed for a very brief second before returning to the glass in her hand, which appeared to hold red wine.

I was instantly drawn to her and walked up to the bar with the hope of engaging in a conversation. As I neared her, she turned instantly, almost as if she expected me to walk up to her, and our arms brushed against each other, almost spilling her wine.

"Oops, sorry," she said, looking genuinely apologetic.

"That's ok," I said. "My fault."

"How is that?" she asked and laughed.

I was stumped. Her confidence drew me closer to her. "To be honest, I really don't know." We both laughed. "Hi, I'm Dinesh."

She smiled and returned to her drink.

I looked at her expectantly, but she cast a glance askance at the assembled guests, tapping her well-manicured fingers on the glass she was holding. I felt awkward and didn't know what to say. For the first time in so many years, I felt tongue-tied.

"Are you waiting for my name?" she asked.

"Yes," I blurted. "Isn't that how it's supposed to flow?"

"Just messing with you. I'm Shayna."

The conversation appeared a bit forced, almost as if she was humoring me. "You here by yourself?"

"Yes," I replied.

"This is so boring. I hate these kinds of evenings. I'd rather be in a library with my books. My parents are in the civil services, and they drag me along to all these invites, whether I like it or not."

"Where are they now?"

"Oh, there they are, with the High Commissioner and his wife. I'm so glad that you..." her voice trailed off.

"I'm here because of some high-contact friends I have. They like to pass on invites they receive, and I'm usually the one they dump them on. Since I'm alone, they feel these invites will help me feel less lonely." I laughed. She continued to listen intently.

I looked at her closely. She was not beautiful in the literal sense, but she was attractive and had a disarming style that seemed genuine and sincere. She laughed a lot, and her eyes were bright and vulnerable.

As the evening wore on, we found ourselves engaged in conversations ranging from disease to divinity; it felt almost like long-lost friends meeting after a long time. She was so easy to converse with, and I was beginning to wonder if there was such a thing as the cliché of love at first sight.

Each exchange revealed the depth of her intellect. She was pursuing her master's from Wharton Business School to be more equipped to start a business of her own one day.

"I don't want to be working for anyone," she had stated emphatically. "But it's quite a challenge, juggling studies and these ridiculous social obligations—except this one…" her voice trailed off.

"I can only imagine. But I'm sure you can do it."

We headed to the food section and helped ourselves. She introduced me to her parents as our paths crossed at the buffet table. Her father appeared distracted, and her mother was over-indulgent and probing. They soon moved away as they spotted another guest they knew, and I almost heard Shayna heave a sigh of relief. She smiled as she saw me looking at her.

We exchanged more thoughts as the evening wore on, and at the end of it all, I mustered up enough courage to ask her for her number.

"My parents are done with their formalities, I think," she said, glancing at the other end of the large dining hall. "I'll have to leave now. I really did enjoy chatting with you, but I need to go."

My heart sank.

"When do you return to the US?" I asked, feeling sorrowful at her impending departure.

"In three months," she said as she placed her glass of water at the bar counter.

"Would you like to meet?" I asked.

"Yes, of course. I was waiting for you to ask," she said, laughing. "I have to go now. Here's my number." So saying, she asked for my phone. I unlocked it and handed it to her. She quickly punched in the number and joined her family. As she left, she turned back and waved to me with a smile.

Never had three hours passed so quickly. I walked out, trying hard not to be seen following her. It was in vain. She had already left.

Days passed, and then my phone rang. My heart skipped a beat as I read her name on the screen.

"Hi, stranger. I bet you were waiting for my call."

"Of course, I was," I said, not embarrassed to state the honest truth.

"Then you should have called."

"Yes, but…"

"Achcha, listen. I have to go to this book club that I'm a member of. Want to join me? It's this Saturday at 10."

"Sure," I said almost instinctively. Had I appeared too desperate, I wondered, but it was too late.

"Good. Can you pick me up at 9:30 from my place? I'll text you my address."

"Cool."

This turned out to be the beginning of the numerous times we got to be together. Our meetings became more frequent, from the book clubs to walks in Lodhi Gardens, to movies, lunches, and dinners. Our calls went late into the night, sometimes through to the next morning. It was inexplicable how we had grown so close in such a short period.

The opposites in our personalities bore the answer to the unfolding of our relationship. She, an affluent girl with an intellect born of her well-heeled, academically oriented family of civil servants, and me, with the vulnerability of a person trying to find his footing in a society to which I did not belong.

What began as an unplanned encounter at a diplomatic mission party had blossomed into a love story that unfolded without a script, guided by the whims of serendipity and the unyielding force of our shared destiny.

Chapter 8

In the weeks and months that followed, there was no physicality except for the inadvertent touching of our fingers as we walked side by side or our arms as we sat beside each other at the PVR multiplex.

As the day of Shayna's departure drew near, a heavy weight settled in the pit of my stomach, the impending farewell looming over us like a dark cloud. We sat together in the dimly lit living room, our hands intertwined, both silently dreading the moment when words would fail us and we would be forced to say goodbye.

Shayna's eyes were brimming with unshed tears as she turned to me, her voice trembling with emotion. "I can't believe this day is finally here," she whispered, her words barely audible above the pounding of my heart.

I reached out to brush a stray tear from her cheek, my own eyes misting over with unspoken sorrow. "I know," I murmured, my voice choked with emotion. "It feels like just yesterday we met, and now…"

"And now," Shayna echoed softly, her gaze locking with mine in a silent plea for understanding. "I don't want to leave you, but I have to. My studies, my future ... they're calling me back to the States."

Her words hung heavy in the air, each syllable a painful reminder of the distance that would soon separate us. I felt a lump form in my throat as I struggled to find the right words to express the depth of my emotions, to convey the ache of knowing that she would soon be gone.

"I understand," I said finally, my voice barely above a whisper. "I understand, but that doesn't make it any easier."

Shayna nodded, her lips trembling with suppressed emotion. "I know," she whispered, her voice barely audible. "But we'll make it work, won't we? We'll find a way to bridge the distance, to keep our love alive across the miles, wont we?"

A surge of determination washed over me as I met her gaze, my heart swelling with a newfound resolve. "Yes," I said firmly, my voice ringing with conviction. "Yes, we will.."

With that, we embraced, clinging to each other as if our lives depended on it, unwilling to let go of the precious moments we had shared together. I turned and kissed her and she reciprocated.

As Shayna's taxi pulled away, carrying her away from me and toward an uncertain future, I knew that our love would endure, a beacon of hope shining bright amidst the darkness of separation.

I couldn't help but marvel at the suddenness with which we had grown closer. A chance meeting had blossomed into a deep and profound connection, one that seemed to defy logic and reason. It was as if fate had intervened, weaving our lives together with unexpected twists and turns.

The sense of loss, now a reality, was to remain as a constant reminder of the fragility of our love in the face of uncertainty.

The distance between Shayna at Wharton and myself navigating through life was a formidable challenge, yet our love proved to be stronger than any miles between us. Despite the physical distance, our connection remained unwavering, a testament to the depth of our bond.

Chapter 9

"Moolchand, Bhogal, Neoda, Neoda, Neoda!" yelled the conductor of a Blue Line bus, banging on its side for emphasis.

An urchin selling peanuts tried to hop onto the bus but was almost kicked in the face by the conductor. "Get lost, you son of a bitch!" he shouted, laughing loudly. His laughter was quickly echoed by his friends and a few passengers on the bus. What made them think they could act this way? Was it arrogance or a misguided attempt to appear tough? Being tough isn't about being abrasive or abusive, or kicking an urchin in the face—it's about recognizing your inner strength and drawing on it in times of adversity. My thoughts began to drift…

The urchin, likely in his teens, barely managed to avoid falling under the bus's wheels. He didn't look surprised or upset. This must have been an everyday occurrence for him. The city had likely stripped him of whatever self-respect or confidence he once had. Constant abuse, with no way to escape it or change how the world saw him, must have left him frustrated and hopeless.

The sight of him triggered a cascade of memories, like dominoes falling one after another. It wasn't the first time this had happened, but each time, the unsettling sense of familiarity gripped me. A memory from Saket floated at the edges of my mind. I knew it was connected, but the specifics were frustratingly out of reach, obscured by forgetfulness. No matter how hard I tried, I couldn't recall what had happened or why it mattered.

And now, as I stood at the bus stop, the image of the urchin stirred those buried thoughts again. something about the way he moved—the tilt of his head or the glint in his eye—stirred an old, dormant recollection.

The pieces of the memory remained scattered, disjointed. It felt as if my mind was shielding me from something, protecting me from a truth I wasn't ready to face. Yet the persistence of the memory ate into me, refusing to be ignored.

I shook off the thoughts momentarily and lit a cigarette from a nearby kiosk. I looked back at the urchin as he dragged his bare feet across the hot pavement to reclaim his spot by the footpath. People waiting for the bus casually stole peanuts from his basket without paying. He didn't say a word. His dirt-smeared eyes were glazed, but there was a faint hope that someone would eventually pay.

When the boy approached me, holding out his peanuts, I felt a pang of sympathy. Despite his ragged clothes and dusty skin, his eyes carried a brightness far beyond his years, shaped by the harshness of his life.

"Uncle, want to buy some peanuts?" he asked, his voice a mix of frustration and weariness.

I glanced down at him. "How much?" I asked, already knowing I wouldn't refuse him.

"Five rupees for 100 grams," he said, a tinge of uncertainty in his voice.

I nodded. "Give me 200 grams." Relief flickered across his face as he prepared a paper cone filled with peanuts. I handed him a twenty-rupee note, but his face clouded with hesitation.

"Uncle, I don't have change," he admitted.

"Keep the change," I said firmly.

His eyes widened in disbelief, and he mumbled, "Thank you, Uncle." But then he paused, as though struck by a thought.

"Uncle, can you give me two ten-rupee notes instead?" he asked hesitantly.

Curious, I handed him the two notes. His face lit up as he explained, "I'll give ten rupees to my father—he's too old to walk—and keep the other ten to buy a storybook."

A lump formed in my throat. I wasn't sure if he could read or if the book was just a way to escape into its colors, but his simple request resonated deeply.

As I watched him disappear into the crowd, I couldn't shake the feeling that I had received far more than I had given.

Driving away, I caught sight of another boy trying to squeeze the last drop of juice from a discarded tetra pack. The urchin lingered in my mind. He reminded me of someone from years ago—someone whose innocence had been stolen. But who? The memory refused to surface.

Later that evening, my old school friend Tapas arrived, as always, two hours late. We laughed over drinks, reminisced about the past, and debated India's charm versus his life in the U.S.

When the night wound down, we took an Uber back. As the car navigated Delhi's battered roads, Tapas exclaimed, "Man, these roads are terrible!"

"You can always walk," I joked, a touch of weariness in my voice.

At a traffic light, he noticed a girl with her hands over the headlights of a BMW. I explained, "She's not fiddling with the lights; she's trying to stay warm."

Without hesitation, Tapas handed her money. As she disappeared into the night, I realized that even the smallest gestures could illuminate the darkest moments. And in the quiet of the Uber, I resolved to dig deeper into the memories that had haunted me all day.

Chapter 10

In the quaint village of Kerala, nestled amidst the lush greenery and swaying coconut palms, lived an elderly couple, Raghavan and Meenakshi. Having spent the prime years of their lives working hard and raising their only son in the bustling city, they decided to retire to their roots.

Raghavan found immense joy in the simple pleasures of farming. The earth beneath his feet, the aroma of wet soil during the monsoons, and the rhythmic sounds of nature became the backdrop of his retirement. He would spend hours tending to the crops, feeling a deep connection to the land that had been in his family for generations.

Despite the idyllic surroundings, Raghavan could not shake the longing for me, his only son, Dinesh. The distance weighed heavy on Raghavan's heart, and the vast fields echoed with his silent wishes for his family to be reunited in the place where their roots run deep. My parents found solace in the simplicity of their village life, but the desire to reunite with his extended family lingered in the air like a soft melody.

He made frequent trips to the bustling metropolis, hoping to bridge the gap that miles and time had created. He would arrive with a heart full of stories from the village, eager to share the warmth of their ancestral home with me.

However, caught in the relentless pursuit of success, I often found himself entangled in meetings, deadlines, and the perpetual rush that defined his days. My father, standing at the doorstep of my world, felt a sense of helplessness as their meetings were brief and fleeting.

Each time Raghavan extended an invitation for me to return home, my response was a promise for 'next time'. The promise of reunification lingered in the air but as the years unfolded, the promises of 'next time' accumulated, becoming a silent echo in the corridors of their familial bond. The trips to Delhi became a pilgrimage of love, a journey that symbolized Raghavan's undying affection and his unwavering hope for a future where I would return for good.

As the years passed, my father's health began to decline. The wear and tear of a lifetime's hard work manifested in the form of ailments, and Meenakshi became the silent witness to her husband's quiet battles. Yet, Raghavan held strong, not just for himself but for the dream he nurtured in his heart—the dream of holding his grandchild in his arms, feeling the warmth of a new generation that would carry forward the legacy of their family.

In the evenings, as the sun dipped below the horizon, Raghavan and Meenakshi would sit on the porch, gazing at the stars that adorned the Kerala sky. He often spoke to Meenakshi about his wish for me, now settled in the corporate world, to return with his own family and breathe life into the old house.

My father would visit me as often as he could. He refused to change with the times. A man who spent his entire life in government service, was clinging to a simple, non-pompous existence. Travel still meant a ride on a DTC bus, and fixing a pressure cooker from a shanty store in Sarojini Nagar.

"I will come to pick you up. What time is the train, what is the train number, and which station?"

"No need for you to come. I can come in DTC, and you can pick me up from AIIMS or something that is more convenient for you."

"No, no, I will come."

The weather was tumultuous, and I had to abandon any plan of taking my own car. Buying a car is one thing; driving and, more importantly, parking it in New Delhi Railway Station is another. After driving to my friend's place in Saket, where I had last visited in an aborted attempt to purchase a flat, I hailed a taxi. The driver, unfazed by the defects, navigated through the flooded streets, stereo blaring the choicest raunchy renditions.

He had not bothered to activate the wipers, wiping the raindrops manually, blissfully humming a song. In the world of jugaad, why fix what works, even if it is unconventional? As the rain subsided, he dropped the wiper back inside the car, content with his makeshift solution.

Arriving at the platform, I got my platform ticket and made my way to Platform no 9. As the train arrived, I craned my neck to spot my father in bogey no 14. He disembarked slowly, his frailty starkly contrasting with his past life as a Cabinet Secretary. A once-healthy man, now weakened by multiple surgeries, faced the harsh realities of life post-retirement.

As he got down from the train, I helped him with the baggage, an old duffel bag that he had been carrying around for years and which he refused to part with or change.

"How is everything beta?" he asked as I hugged him.

"Moving along," I said and he smiled. All these years had got him accustomed to that response.

"How is work treating you?"

"Not too bad," I replied and we proceeded to walk toward the main exit point.

We exchanged greetings, but unspoken words lingered between us. The hardships he endured were etched on his face—the city had taken more from him than it had given. My dad was a contradiction of the fact that good deeds beget good outcomes. He had endured all this but had not wavered. For me, it was hard to comprehend that all this was happening in the lifetime of one individual.

"Sirjee, taxi, hotel aur koi cheez…" enquired a cab driver as we exited the main gate. As I was walking ahead with my Dad following me, the fair presumption was that I was a visitor and therefore would need transport.

I looked back for my dad but the banter continued. "Taxi, want taxi…good guest house…..all facilities." I looked at him and he had a slight grin on his face. "We have arrangement to cater to every taste sirjee…"

My father was still a fair distance away, walking slowly down the stairs. "No, thanks." I retorted angrily.

"You will get a good deal," he continued.

"Didn't you hear me say no, you jerk!" I replied in an angry tone.

I looked around and spotted a taxi parked near the road with an old man sitting inside making no attempt to market his services. I called out to him, placed the luggage in the boot and helped my father get in. As the car maneuvered through the chaotic streets, I couldn't help but feel a surge of protectiveness towards my father. Yet, as he settled into the seat beside me, a small smile of relief graced his features, a silent acknowledgment of the respite that the car afforded him.

I glanced out the window, the scene outside a dizzying blur of motion and noise. The filth and stench of the unkempt garbage bins mingled with the leering stares of the auto-rickshaw drivers, their eyes following the passing women.

It had stopped raining and there was less dust all around. The overflowing drains bore testimony to the fact that the rains would be remembered for many more days even if it stopped raining. As the taxi meandered its way through the traffic and jumped the red light, an autorickshaw passed me. I thought I recognized the face in the auto but was not sure. We continued to rumble through the potholed roads and waited as a traffic police officer motioned the traffic to stop. I wondered why he did so and moments later I saw a convoy of Ambassador cars pass through the Connaught Place outer circle area. A VIP movement and the city comes to a standstill. Some minutes later, we were back on our way.

The autorickshaw which I had noticed, was parked a couple of cars ahead of me. As the taxi glided past the auto-rickshaw, a chill ran down my spine. There he was—the same man I had encountered at the railway station's exit, the one who had propositioned a mysterious 'good deal' to me. His presence raised an immediate sense of unease, like an unwelcome specter from the recent past.

Beside him in the auto-rickshaw sat another man, nonchalantly chewing betel leaves. What truly unsettled me was the sight of a young girl, no older than 14, huddled between the two men. Her eyes, brimming with unshed tears, spoke volumes, their silent plea echoing in the recesses of my mind.

As the taxi carried us further away from the scene, I found myself consumed by an unsettling sense of déjà vu. Why did her presence stir such a tumult of emotions within me? I couldn't shake the feeling that there was more to this encounter than met the eye, that beneath the surface lay a labyrinth of secrets and hidden motives.

As the taxi rumbled on, each passing mile seemed to deepen the mystery of the sight that I had just witnessed. The young girl, petrified, sandwiched between two burly men each one more repulsive than the other and as the cityscape blurred past the window, I couldn't help but wonder what other mysteries lay hidden in the shadows, waiting to be unearthed.

Soon enough, the taxi groaned to a stop. I held my Dad's hand and escorted him up the flight of stairs pausing at every 5 steps for him to regain his breath. We reached the living room as he sat down on the couch. I left to prepare tea for him.

"Are you okay, Dad?"

He simply smiled. He was not okay. After a while or so, as he sipped his tea, he seemed to regain his strength somewhat and made light conversation.

"I do need to meet with Mr. Bajaj tomorrow."

"Sure, I will arrange that, Dad," I said.

"You could drop me at the nearest bus stop, and I will figure my way."

"I will take you there myself. Don't worry."

He smiled. "You have a good house here, and I'm glad that you have settled down well. I guess I do not have to worry about you anymore."

"You should never have to worry, Dad."

I did not even, for a minute, imagine that my response would prove to be prophetic.

In me, my father had dreamt of a life that he had not been able to live. Educated in a Public school in Delhi with the mannerisms of a Delhiite was all that he was not. A subdued and subservient Government servant had found amazement in the contradictions that my personality revealed. My progress through the Corporate ladder, my mannerisms and the way I would conduct myself in a social setting were diametrically opposed to the lifestyle that he had led and he found that endearing in a twisted way. As a student, I had excelled in practically all my subjects and that was a badge of honor that he wore with aplomb, never missing an opportunity to boast about with his colleagues at work and beyond.

I related to my father more like a friend with whom I could share my wildest thoughts, hopes and dreams knowing deep down that he would try his darndest to help fulfill. His struggles with finances to help keep my dreams afloat was not unknown to me but I could do little to help share the pain he experienced with the separation that life brought about.

His poignant pilgrimage to Delhi, a city he had dedicated his life to in more ways than one, was merely an excuse to rid his heart of the aching pain he experienced each time he did not find me next to him in Kerala. It was a soulful reassurance, a pilgrimage of love to see his son and the family he held dear.

My father, who had carried the weight of responsibility with grace, would never have to worry anymore.

As the city slumbered, my father, the pillar of our family, breathed his last in the embrace of sleep. Delhi, the city that had witnessed the chronicles of his life, now became the silent witness to his concluding chapter. In ways more profound than I could understand, my father's journey had come full circle, reminiscent of a salmon that had tirelessly swum upstream against the relentless tide, only to find its journey's end at the very source.

Chapter 11

"Let's have breakfast in Old Delhi." That was Manoj, my partner in crime.

"Sure, let's do it," I said, locking in our plan to meet at Nirula's Pot Pourri at 8 AM.

The idea felt like a flashback from our college days—a shared dream to savor Old Delhi's legendary breakfasts on a quiet Sunday morning. Years had passed since college, but the allure of Old Delhi's ghee-drenched delicacies and Karim's famous Burra kebabs, the kind that could humble even KFC, hadn't dimmed. Neither had the darker shadows of the place: GB Road, Delhi's infamous red-light district, lurking just out of sight.

The fun nature that Manoj exuded appealed to me no end. We were of the same age and he was the kind of businessman who thrived in the space where the lines between right and wrong often blurred. He had a knack for survival, an innate street-smartness that allowed him to survive with aplomb in the city where the weak get devoured in no time. He was blessed with the gift of gab and he could hold forth on anything from disease to divinity, spinning yarns with an ease that often left his audience both impressed and wary As a true-blue Delhiite, he had mastered the art of speaking his way out of trouble—a skill that had served him well in both his personal and professional life.

Manoj had slid effortlessly into his father's cargo packaging business after finishing his MBA, a natural progression that felt more like destiny than effort. But it wasn't long before he expanded the family trade, diversifying into cargo transportation and cold storage transporting frozen meat across the country but his appearance did little to match the image of success he cultivated. He was average-looking and had an awkward sense of style that seemed to reflect his nature. Branded clothes hung on him in mismatched disarray, yet this lack of polish only added to his peculiar charm, making him appear grounded and relatable.

Manoj was the life of any gathering. Outgoing and quick-witted, he had a way of putting people at ease, his jokes—often self-deprecating or bordering on poor taste—eliciting laughter despite their simplicity. But beneath the camaraderie, there was always a subtle dissonance. I could never fully trust him. There was something about the way he navigated relationships, always with an eye on how they could benefit him, that set my instincts on edge. Yet, I had no choice but to seek his company. My quest demanded a certain kind of ally, someone who could navigate the gray areas I often shied away from, and Manoj fit the role perfectly.

Our bond had been forged while we sat in the classroom completing our MB together. However, it was only after graduation that we became friends. I was the conservative one, focused on rules and boundaries, while Manoj was the quintessential hustler, thriving on bending the same rules to his advantage. Despite these differences, we found ourselves drawn to each other. I still remember the day he showed up unannounced at the Shroff Clinic while I was recovering from a minor eye surgery. That gesture, unexpected and oddly touching, cemented our friendship. It was a guarded bond, though, marked by unspoken reservations on my part and an almost predatory curiosity on his.

Manoj's attitude toward relationships was as pragmatic as his approach to business. For him, connections were assets, to be nurtured and, when necessary, leveraged. With me and a couple of other friends, he maintained a semblance of genuine camaraderie, always present when needed, but I couldn't shake the feeling that even these bonds were calculated. He was not vested in my madness—the quest that had consumed me—but he seemed intrigued by it. Perhaps he saw an opportunity for excitement or a chance to add another story to his repertoire. Perhaps he genuinely wanted to help me find closure. Whatever his reasons, Manoj's involvement brought a sense of unpredictability to my journey.

At home, Manoj was a paradox. Despite his modern, outgoing persona, he held deeply conservative views about family and gender roles. Women, in his eyes, were meant to remain in the kitchen and bear children—a belief that clashed starkly with the progressive attitudes he displayed in his social circle. It was a duality that puzzled and frustrated me, a reminder of the contradictions that defined him.

Together, we made an odd pair. Where he exuded confidence and street smarts, I was cautious and methodical. His ability to charm his way through obstacles often left me marveling, even as I questioned his motives. We spent countless hours bullshitting around, cracking terrible jokes, and reveling in the shared absurdity of life.

Manoj's role in my quest was both essential and enigmatic. He guided me through the labyrinthine paths I was too wary to tread alone, his street-smart instincts complementing my more rigid approach. At times, I wondered if he found purpose in my mission, if helping me allowed him to tap into something larger than himself. Or perhaps it was all just another adventure for him, a way to add a dash of excitement to his life.

Whatever the truth, Manoj remained an enigma. A fun-loving guy, a loyal friend in moments that mattered. He was the kind of person you couldn't entirely trust yet couldn't entirely dismiss either.

True to form, Manoj arrived fashionably late. By then, my anticipation had brewed into restlessness. We took a cycle rickshaw—cars weren't made for Old Delhi's maze of alleys. As we approached GB Road, memories came rushing back. Seven years ago, I'd been here with Indrani. Her absence now felt strange, like a missing piece of the puzzle. The street, though, was unchanged with its hardware shops below, brothels perched above.

A woman from a rickety balcony called out, "Come here, hero," her voice cutting through the din. I glanced up. A dark-complexioned woman waved, her presence a jarring reminder of this place's harsh realities.

And then it hit me. The girl from seven years ago. How had I forgotten her? She couldn't have been more than seven or eight years old, just a child. An old man had mentioned she was "being prepared for the trade." The thought made my stomach churn. Seven years. Could she still be here? Where else could she go?

"Why am I thinking about this now?" I muttered under my breath. But something in me had snapped. I needed to know what had happened to her.

We reached Chawri Bazaar, stopping at Anupam Sweet Shop for breakfast. Over chai and jalebis, I told Manoj about the girl and the story I'd once shared with Indrani. He looked surprised—not by the story, but by the fact that I still remembered.

"This is common, man," he said, shaking his head. "What are you trying to do? Be a hero now?"

"Can we go there?" I asked, almost pleading.

He stared at me like I'd lost my mind. "Are you serious? Seven years, bro! She's probably..." he paused "not there anymore. Why dig this up?"

"Closure," I said simply.

Manoj sighed. "These places aren't permanent. Girls get moved around like inventory. They're nomads."

"You know this area, Manoj. Can't you ask around?"

He laughed bitterly. "These aren't exactly my kind of people. Do you even remember her name?"

I didn't. The realization stung. I had ignored the moment when she'd told me, too caught up in everything else. "No, but I'd recognize her."

"You're delusional," Manoj said, throwing up his hands. "What? You think they'll line up girls for you to ID? And then what? You'll take her home? Fix her life? This isn't a movie."

His frustration was evident, but so was his loyalty. After a long pause, he asked, "Why not ask Indrani for help?"

"I don't even know where she is. She hasn't returned my calls. And besides, this isn't her kind of thing."

Manoj exhaled loudly. "Fine. But you know this is pointless, right? Without a name..."

His words trailed off as the waiter brought forth the bill for the food we had consumed. I reached for it, just as my eyes also caught a movie poster across the street that had come half undone from the decrepit wall it was pasted on at the other side of the road. It wasn't the actor that caught my attention but the title of the film. A memory ignited like a spark in the darkness and I couldn't help but thrust my fist upwards as a sign of victory.

"Jannat. Her name is Jannat." I almost shouted.

Chapter 12

Manoj was a local through and through. His hardware store in the heart of Chawri Bazaar wasn't just a business—it was a gateway to the pulse of the market. Every nut, bolt, and tool he sold connected him to the lives of merchants and traders. People knew him, and he knew them, which meant doors often opened for him. But whether those doors extended to the brothels of GB Road was anyone's guess.

He sighed and looked at me, his reluctance clear. "Fine. Let's get this over with."

We stopped the rickshaw just before 11 a.m. and walked toward one of the kothas.

"You sure about this?" Manoj asked again, exasperated.

"I'm sure," I said, my impatience bubbling over.

The crowd thinned as we reached a steep flight of stairs. Manoj glanced around, then led the way. Halfway up, a pimp appeared, blocking our path.

"What do you want?" he barked.

I tried to explain. "We're looking for someone. A girl named Jannat."

The pimp cut me off. "This isn't a sightseeing spot. You want a girl, you pay. No free tours."

Manoj jumped in. "My friend met a girl here years ago. She was just a kid then. He's back to see if she's still here."

The pimp stared at us, the aggression in his eyes unwavering. "Five thousand rupees or get lost."

I hesitated, glancing at Manoj.

"Four thousand," I countered.

He smirked, sensing desperation. "Fine. But don't waste my time."

Money exchanged hands, and he led us down a narrow hallway, curtains serving as flimsy barriers to rooms on either side. A glance through one pulled-back curtain revealed a grim scene. Girls huddled together, fear etched on their faces. The air was thick with despair.

"This place is hell," I muttered.

Manoj nudged me as the pimp stopped at a door. "Jannat's in the next compartment," he said with a sly grin.

My heart pounded in my chest as he reached for the curtain, the sound of the rings sliding along the rod sharp against the silence. A part of me wanted to stop him, to prepare myself for whatever lay behind it, but I couldn't move. A part of me was not prepared to face any disappointment that was always an option. The curtain fell away, revealing a dimly lit room, and there she sat, a young girl huddled near the bed.

Her thin arms wrapped around her knees, her face pale and shadowed by exhaustion. Her wide eyes locked onto mine for a fleeting moment, filled with fear and something else I couldn't quite place. Then, as if weighed down by the acceptance of what lay ahead, she looked away, her gaze sinking to the floor in quiet resignation.

For a heartbeat, hope clung to me, fragile and desperate. Was it her? Could it be her? I stepped closer, my breath shallow, until the realization hit.

"It's not her," I said, my voice barely above a whisper.

The pimp shrugged. "There's another one. Might be her. Who knows?"

We moved to another compartment. He peeked inside, then motioned for me to enter.

"Is this the one?"

I stepped in, and there she was. A girl, no older than fourteen, her jet-black hair falling in waves around her face. Time had hardened her features, but beneath the surface, there was a flicker of familiarity.

"Yes, Yes, Yes," I whispered. "This is her."

Manoj's expression softened as he caught my gaze. Relief and disbelief played across his face. For seven years, she'd been a shadow in my mind, a memory too painful to revisit. And now, here she was, alive, but trapped in a nightmare.

"Bolo, Seth. Threesome or twosome?" she asked, her tone flat, devoid of emotion.

I could tell that she had been 'initiated' into the trade for some time. The child-like innocence was fast waning but it was still there. She did not seem to recognize me and I did not try to help her recollect. I looked at Manoj as both of us did not know how to proceed next. I looked around the room. There was a portable TV in one corner of the room with a V-shaped antenna jutting out from the back. A small table lay parked with many books kept on top of it. A shelf on top of the table had a picture. A picture of her and another boy. Next to the picture were cheap Barbie dolls. It was evident that she had tried to dress up as Barbie. I walked up to the table to see the books in which she was interested.

"Bolo Seth. I do not have time to waste. Others are waiting."

I continued towards the table and saw that these were `Amar Chitra Katha' books. This was one side of her. A side that was her own, to be shared with no one. The side she wanted to show was not what I wanted to see. On one side of the wall lay the evidence to prove that she was still very much a child. On the other side was a bed with posters of naked women cello-taped on the wall. Two sides of the same coin and each one is so much in contrast. One side depicted childhood and the other side depicted the state that she was in. In the middle, where we sat, was the painful balance.

"You may not remember that many years ago I met you with a friend of mine." She looked at me lost and I was beginning to understand the futility of my efforts. "I...err, we wanted to talk to you and hear your story. What are you going through and is there any way we can help?"

"Why me? There are many like me out there. Are you trying to get me into trouble?"

"Never would we think of that. Do you think we would put ourselves in so much trouble just to put you in danger? The pimp was almost going to kill us. The day I saw you many years ago, there was an emotional chord you struck with me. I cannot explain what it was. You are right. There will be many others but I feel that I know you in a twisted way and want to see if I can make a difference in your life. Help you in any way I can. You were only 7 when I first saw you..." I could not continue as I choked on my words.

Manoj placed his hand on my shoulder.

She agreed to talk to us after much persuasion. Her unfortunate story unfolded as a series of missed opportunities. She was from West Bengal. Her parents, with a meager income, had children to support. It was a difficult task to survive.

She said that she was abducted at the age of 7. A relative had taken her to, what he called, a meeting with her long-lost family members and she had gone along with him. What she did not know was the price at which she had been sold to the man by her parents. Jannat recalled her past.

"I was sold in Sonagachi in Kolkata. A girl was a burden while my younger brother with a speech defect stayed on as nobody found him to be a useful purchase. After I was brought here, I was taught to sing and dance. After almost a year, the malkeen's babu assaulted me to prepare me for this trade. After a few months, I was formally initiated. One day there was a police raid in the brothel where I was living, and I was taken into police custody."

"Then what happened?" I asked unable to hide my impatience.

Suddenly she bared her legs and showed a deep scar. "I was put behind bars. There at midnight a police officer came and tried to squeeze me out of the lock-up. He could not squeeze me out, my legs got entangled in the iron bars. My legs were injured and were bleeding profusely but he did not care. I was shouting but there was no one to listen."

Jannat went on with her tale of horror. "I have been staying here for almost 7 years. When there were no clients, we were pushed into a cage and locked in."

I could not take it anymore and motioned to Manoj to leave.

"Sorry, Seth. You will not complain to Madam, will you?" she enquired as we were leaving with fear writ large on her face.

"No, we will not. Don't worry." I replied trying very hard to cover the film that was forming in my eyes.

She walked towards the bed, lifted the thin dirty mattress, and took out a condom pack. She quickly ripped it open, took out two condoms, and threw the silver foils on the floor.

"They look for proof. An unsatisfied customer means loss of repeat business. We have to do it whether we like it or not." Having said that she walked across to the toilet and flushed the unused condom down but left the condom cover lying on the floor. That was her evidence of survival and life.

"Don't you want to get out of here?" I asked abruptly unable to come to terms with the fact that she would have to live the best years of her life with that fear and abuse without any escape in sight.

"It's too late now bhaiyya and I am very scared." She said addressing me for the first time as her brother.

"Why is it too late now?"

"I think they are now looking to sell me off as I have outlived my shelf life here." She sounded so robotic as she said that. "I overheard the maalkin talk about me being taken away to make place for a younger one."

"Younger than fourteen?" I thought and winced.

"It is simply a matter of time and I will be just another statistic. I wanted to study and be a doctor but that dream is going to die with me, I think."

"Don't lose hope, I will.."

"Bhaiyya, please. Can you…?" she started, her eyes betraying the hope that was still submerged within the deep recesses of her mind. The pimp had returned and was standing outside the room waiting to pull the curtain aside.

"You don't plan to spend the whole day here, do you?" he said as he pulled the curtain aside.

I was hoping he had not heard what was being said. He looked around and smiled as he saw the 2 used condom packs on the floor.

"You guys are real professionals." he chuckled as he winked at the girl who turned her face away.

Manoj was the first to exit as he pretended to adjust his crotch to lend credibility to the encounter we just had. The pimp followed and I turned to have one last look at her before making my way past the pimp to the corridor.

She was still looking at me. She caught my eye and said `Amake banchao.'

'You are right.' The pimp responded looking at the girl and nodding in agreement at the imagined expletive that she had thrown at us.

As we stepped out into the dimly lit corridors of the hardware market, I couldn't shake off the unsettling feeling that lingered from our encounter with the girl. The pimp, ever watchful, guided us along, ensuring we didn't linger a moment longer than necessary. It was as if he had an invisible leash around us, pulling us along with each step.

My mind raced with questions, trying to decipher the girl's puzzling behavior. Why had she cursed us as we were leaving? We were only trying to be kind to her, yet her words stung like a slap in the face. Had I misjudged the situation entirely? Was I naive to think I could offer her help in any meaningful way?

I couldn't shake the feeling that there was more to her outburst than met the eye. Perhaps she was under the thumb of the pimp, forced to act a certain way in his presence. Or maybe there were deeper reasons behind her anger, reasons I couldn't even begin to fathom.

She had started to say something before the pimp arrived, her words hanging in the air like an unfinished melody. But as soon as he entered, she fell silent, her eyes darting nervously between us. And then, with a venomous glare, she cursed us, her words cutting through the tension like a knife.

We made our way through the busy bylanes and withdrew money from the only HDFC ATM before we started to look for a rickshaw. The pimp had ensured his payment and we were left with no money for the day ahead.

"What a day man" exclaimed Manoj as he settled into the cycle rikshaw with me.

"I am never coming here again," I said.

"What? What happened? I know what you are thinking buddy but it is not what you think it to be. You will surely want to return and return soon." Manoj replied.

I looked at him. His face betrayed concern and he appeared very thoughtful almost trying to come to terms with what he had just heard.

"I don't understand. You were there. Is everything ok?' I asked.

"No, I guess not." He muttered still appearing distracted as if he was trying to undo the knots in his mind. "I am concerned about the girl. God knows that there are probably hundreds like her and we obviously cannot be looking at only one. However, this is the one we have come to know and if we were to help one then maybe there is hope."

"What brought about this change bro? I am glad that you are thinking like a human now but I am not sure if she deserves any help though. She is an ungrateful person and it is probably her circumstances that have made her out to be what she is. There was no reason for her to curse us as we were leaving. You heard it, didn't you?"

"I heard it, my friend and probably clearer than you did." he said, "She did not curse us."

"Of course, she did." I countered.

"No, she did not buddy. She said *amake bachao*. 'Save me'.

I very quickly realized that as we delved deeper into my madness, Manoj's presence became both a comfort and a reminder of the unpredictable nature of the path I, and he in turn, had been inexorably thrust into.

Chapter 13

"Aman," he said out loud as the boy in front of her struggled to keep his attention focused on the book in front of him. "I will not repeat what I'm telling you."

In the modest living room, the air was thick with both love and unspoken fears. Nilofer, a mere 14-year-old, seemed wise beyond her years, her eyes carrying the weight of experiences that belied her age. She glanced at Aman and called out his name.

Aman smiled, as he only knew too well, that behind the tough exterior that exhibited, she was the most caring girl he knew in this world, somebody who had protected him at all times and t so much pain to make sure that he was able to find meaning in his life, to understand what love and caring truly stood for, understand the basic level of Hindi and even English so that he could get by on a day-to-day basis, to be able to survive in this city. This city can be harsh on people, more so if you cannot speak and Aman was no exception. Aman was dumb and able to utter only some words with great difficulty and in a way that could still not be understood by many.

Shury dudi he uttered and Nilofer smiled as she hugged him. She had taken an instant liking to the boy when he was brought in for the first time by her father. Her father had decided that he would be able to help around the house and in the shop he owned in return for food and a roof over his head. The boy had not resisted.

"How could anything get any worse for me?" he had reasoned with himself. It turned out to be a boon for him as Nilofer took him under her wing instantly with love and affection that he never knew the meaning of.

"Are you okay?" she whispered, crouching beside Aman as he sat curled up on the floor, his small fingers trembling against the torn seam of his sweater. She could see the faint red mark on his arm where her father had grabbed him earlier.

Aman glanced up at her, his dark, round eyes brimming with unshed tears. He opened his mouth to respond, but no words came. They rarely did. His lips moved silently, his frustration and fear palpable.

Nilofer placed a gentle hand on his shoulder. "It's okay, Amu. You don't have to say anything."

He nodded, pressing his face into his knees. She hated seeing him like this, so small and scared, the way she used to feel before she learned to fight back. At such a young age, Aman already bore the weight of too much sadness and too much silence.

"You know what I see when I look at you?" she said softly, sitting cross-legged in front of him. He peeked at her through the curtain of his messy hair.

"I see someone stronger than anyone I know. You don't even need words to tell people who you are. You're brave, Amu. Braver than me."

Aman shook his head furiously, his lips quivering. He raised a hand and tapped his chest twice—his way of saying, "No."

Nilofer sighed and reached for his hand, wrapping her fingers around his small, cold ones. "Yes, you are. Don't let him make you think you're not."

He stared at her, his expression softening. Slowly, he reached into the pocket of his sweater and pulled out the little wooden bird she had given him the week before. He ran his thumb over its wing and held it out to her.

"For me?" she asked, a smile tugging at the corner of her lips.

He nodded, tapping his chest once, then pointing at her. "Ou," he murmured, his voice faint and cracked but determined.

Nilofer's heart swelled, and she bit her lip to keep her tears at bay. "You're my little brother, Amu. No matter what happens, I'm always going to protect you. Okay? Always."

He tilted his head, a flicker of a smile crossing his face. He pressed the wooden bird into her hand and leaned forward, wrapping his arms around her in a tight hug.

In that moment, Nilofer made a promise—to herself and him. Whatever it took, she'd make sure Aman never felt alone again.

She had decided to teach him like her younger brother she never had or like her sister she had lost.

She had been amazed at the speed with which he had grasped languages and numbers. The fact that he could not speak always saddened her and at the same time got her closer to him as a protective shield.

In a household filled with things she didn't approve of, she felt powerless and hopeless, forced to turn a blind eye to maintain her survival and sanity. In Aman, she discovered a glimmer of light in the darkness. Beyond textbooks, Nilofer introduced Aman to the joys of watching TV together, involving him in the daily chores of cleaning and dusting. Their laughter echoed through the small house, becoming a sanctuary amidst the challenges of life.

As a help, he would assist her father at the paan and cigarette store he had and would return home with him in the evening to help out in the kitchen. After that, her father would get busy drinking and go to bed while Nilofer and Aman would spend hours watching TV or just learning new things.

Her, father's outward appearance of respectability belied the darkness that lurked within, a darkness that Nilofer had witnessed first-hand in the aftermath of her mother's passing. She had seen the selfishness and cruelty that lay beneath his facade of propriety, and the memories haunted her. His physical abuse of her younger brother gnawed at her insides and she kept searching for the elusive solution to this vexing issue.

As the two shared their daily lives, Nilofer grappled with an internal struggle. She pondered over how to alter the destiny that awaited Aman—a destiny where he might be cast aside, just as her sister had been. The uncertainty of the future hung heavily in the room, overshadowing the warmth of their makeshift family.

"How can I change the fate that awaits Aman?"

It was late evening, and the two were sitting on the back steps of the house and the faint glow of fireflies lit up the yard. Aman picked at the hem of his worn sweater and Nilofer was quick to sense his unease. She leaned toward him and asked him "Amu. You've been quiet today. Is something wrong?"

Aman shrugged and responded, his voice betraying a certain sense of hesitancy "Nu, m fin." His words come out slow and broken, his speech impairment making each sound deliberate.

Nilofer persisted. "Amu, don't do that. Don't tell me you're okay when I can see you're not. You're picking at your sweater again. You only do that when something's bothering you." She reaches over, stilling his hands with hers.

Aman paused, struggling to find the words, then looked up at her with wide, worried eyes "Abbu … h-he was … m-mad again."

Nilofer's jaw tightened and a flash of anger crossed her face, but she softened it quickly lest Aman get more petrified. "What did he do? Did he say something to you? Did he—". She stopped not wanting to scare him with her fury.

Aman quickly shook his head, his voice trembling "N-not me. Just … y-you. He s-said bad things a-about you."

Tears welled up in his eyes, his words halting as he fought through his frustration with speaking. "I … I c-couldn't … stop him."

Nilofer pulled him closer, her arm instinctively wrapping protectively around his shoulder. "Amu, listen to me. You don't have to stop him. That's not your job, okay? You're a kid. You shouldn't even have to hear the things he says, let alone feel like it's your job to fix them."

"B-but … y-you stop him. F-fur me."

Nilofer's throat tightened, tears pricking her eyes as she realized how much he looked up to her. "Because I'm older, and because I care about you. But Amu … you don't have to protect me. That's my job, okay? I promised I'd keep you safe, and I mean it." She brushed a stray tear from his cheek. "You're my little brother. That's what family does. You and me—we're family because we choose to be. And I'll choose you every time. No matter what. You're stuck with me, got it?"

Aman's lips twitched into the faintest of smiles, his voice steadier now "G-got it."

"Good, and besides, you're way too cool to be my dad's problem. Don't let his words stick, okay? They're not worth it."

"O-okay."

"That's my boy. Now, c'mon. Let's go find some more fireflies before it gets too dark. Ok?"

Aman smiling now, responded "Okay."

Nilofer embraced him yet again. In a way, the fireflies represented their escape from darkness. However, whether she or Aman would banish the darkness in their lives or find a way to overcome their struggles remained to be seen. She did not want Aman to be cast aside as unwanted, just as her father had of her sister some time ago.

Little did she know that the darkness would pave the way for brightness in a way she least expected and it would happen sooner than she had imagined.

Chapter 14

"Oh my God," I exclaimed. "Is that what she said?"

"I'm damn sure, buddy," Manoj replied.

A rickshaw pulled up just then, and I glanced at Manoj without saying another word.

"Let's have a quick smoke," I finally said.

We asked the rickshaw-wallah to wait for us. He happily agreed since he had just finished a trip and needed a break—to rest, grab some water, and light his beedi. We walked toward the nearest paanwallah, who was perched cheerfully on an elevated platform, surrounded by his steel containers. In front of him, a slab of ice-held betel leaves neatly arranged and ready to serve. Behind him, rows of cigarettes lined the shelves, and a basket of chips and snacks dangled from a netted bag.

I needed to calm myself down. Manoj, busy talking on his phone, gestured for me to go ahead.

She wanted to be saved!

"What happened sahib? Is everything ok? You look very worried and disturbed." asked the paanwallah as he spread a thick coat of `katha on the betel leaf he was holding in the palm of his hand.

"Kuch nahin." I said, "Give me a Marlboro Light please."

"Oye chotu, Give a Marlboro Light to the saab here." A young boy opened a pack and handed me a single cigarette with his katha-stained fingers.

The dimly lit street echoed with the soft sounds of the city, creating a surreal backdrop to the intense conversation that had just unfolded. I stood near the paanwallah, a single cigarette hanging between my fingers, the tendrils of smoke weaving a transient dance in the night air. The paanwallah, a man weathered by time but with an air of friendliness, continued to engage in conversation, seemingly unfazed by the gravity of Jannat's harrowing story.

His hands moved with a practiced ease, spreading a thick coat of katha on the betel leaf in his palm, a routine etched by years of experience. As I took a deep drag of the Marlboro Light, the acrid smoke filled my lungs, offering a fleeting respite from the weight of the encounter.

As I took another drag, trying to find solace in the ritual of smoking, I asked the paan wallah, "How long have you been selling paan here?"

"More years than I care to remember." he chuckled, the lines on his face deepening with the laughter. I forced a smile, appreciating the effort to inject a sense of normalcy into the conversation. "I saw you coming out from that direction" he pointed towards the alley we had emerged from. "Did you have a good time?"

I chose to ignore his question, not wanting to delve into the details of the ominous encounter.

"Sorry to be nosey, but you do not seem the type to be visiting places like these, Saab. I'm sure there are better options for you outside this area."

The paanwallah's words hung in the air, a gentle reminder of the incongruity between my presence in this seedy neighborhood and the assumptions about my life. I continued to smoke in silence, the rhythmic inhales and exhales providing a momentary escape from the complexities that surrounded me.

The rickshaw-wallah, having patiently waited, looked up from his beedi and gestured towards us. It was time to leave, to navigate the maze of emotions and unanswered questions that lingered in the aftermath of Jannats revelation. As we embarked on the next leg of our journey, the cityscape unfolded before us, concealing its secrets beneath the surface of its bustling exterior.

Manoj had joined me by then and was now part of the conversation. "No, we had gone to strike a deal with one maalkin for a girl we had met many years ago but they are demanding a very high price. No deal, so we are returning empty-handed," he answered the earlier question from the paanwallah.

"Oh, you are lucky that they were even willing to sell. Most of these girls just vanish, never to be seen again. Do you know her name? Perhaps ay have an idea as everybody comes here and even more share their stories with me. I have been here for a very long time."

"Jannat," I repeated, a sense of determination underlying my words.

The weight of her name hung in the air, and the paanwallah's gaze held a mixture of understanding and a hint of sadness. His eyes widened ever so slightly as if the mere mention of her had conjured a weighty history that lingered in the air. The boy at the back of the shop, who had resumed his work, paused a quiet observer of this unexpected revelation.

There was a palpable silence, broken only by the distant sounds of the city at night. Manoj's stare bore into me, a silent questioning that reflected the gravity of what I had just disclosed. The paanwallah, after a moment that felt like an eternity, nodded slowly.

"I remember Jannat well, although I'm not sure if that is her right name or the name the maalkin gave her. She is a nice girl but she has aged so much over the past so many years."

"Do you know her?" I asked incredulously, eager to unravel the layers of her existence. Manoj's impatience was palpable, his eyes darting anxiously between the paanwallah, me, and the shadows that clung to the corners of the shop.

"Of course, I do," the paanwallah continued, breaking the tension that hung in the air. He sighed, his gaze distant as if staring into the abyss of Jannat's past. "When I look at her, I feel so sad, but these pimps just do not think so. All they can think about is the next customer that she will have to satisfy."

The boy at the back of the shop had abandoned his tasks, drawn into the gravity of our conversation. I looked, offering a smile that remained stoic.

"She comes here sometimes in the morning to buy something or the other, usually paan and cigarettes for her maalkin. I usually end up giving her some sweets." The paanwallah paused, his eyes shifting towards the boy, who now stood at attention. "She's good friends with him," he said, looking at the boy, to which the latter nodded.

"One day she narrated her story to me and I was overcome with grief," The paanwallah said as he sifted his gaze from the boy to me. "I thought I would do something to save her from this mess, but it was not possible. I have to survive here too for my sake and the sake of my family. If any of the pimps find out that I helped with the escape, they will simply kill me and make life impossible for my family. Who are we going to save? Forget about her Sirjee else they will come after you too."

I crushed the butt of my cigarette underfoot as the paanwallah busied himself with another customer. The exchange of money for a brief respite from my thoughts seemed insignificant, and I left a generous tip without bothering to collect the change. The night air clung to the shadows of the narrow alley as I rejoined Manoj on the cycle rickshaw. The rickshaw pulled away, navigating the labyrinthine alleys that seemed to hold the secrets of the night.

Neither of us spoke during the journey back, the rhythmic creaking of the rickshaw wheels punctuating the silence.

Manoj "What's with the boy?"

"Well, seemed very interested in our conversation," I replied, my mind still grappling with the complexities of the night.

"It's just the way he froze when you mentioned Jannats name. Almost like he knew more but could not, for … fear or concern or…" Manoj trailed off, leaving the sentence hanging in the air.

"Well, the guy said that he knew Jannat. It is natural for strangers to react that way when they hear a familiar name, isn't it?" I offered, attempting to dismiss the unease that lingered between us.

"It was not the look of familiarity. It seemed more like a recollection," Manoj concluded, the weight of the unspoken understanding settling between us.

It was well past 1 pm, and the afternoon sun cast long shadows across the bustling city. The day had moved forward, yet the weight of the morning encounter lingered in the recesses of my mind. Manoj and I, each with our own set of errands, parted ways with a promise to meet again soon, continuing the ritual of shared breakfasts and conversations.

As I navigated the busy streets, passing through the iconic India Gate, a sudden wave of realization washed over me. How quickly we had moved on, how easily we had shifted our focus from a girl who had been robbed of her innocence at the tender age of seven. Now, at fourteen, her life had been stolen from her, and the future seemed bleak and devoid of hope.

The police officers, who could have provided a glimmer of hope, had instead shattered any illusions of justice for Jannat. It did not matter whether she was seven or fourteen. The age seemed inconsequential in the face of the atrocities she had endured. Lost in contemplation, I continued my journey through the evolving cityscape. The once mundane tasks at hand now felt inconsequential against the weight of Jannat's struggle. The afternoon sun, casting long shadows on the pavement, seemed to mirror the lingering shadows of her harrowing story etched deep within my memory.

"She had wanted to be saved, but how could I?" I wondered the desperation and hope Jannat had sparked within me shaking my very core. The question echoed in my mind: Was there no escape from the cruel world that had trapped her?

My thoughts were interrupted as I stopped at a traffic signal. The chaos of the city surrounded me—horns blaring, people shouting, life bustling on. Beggars and panhandlers approached, tapping on my window, and smearing sunscreen across my windshield in hopes of earning a few coins. I turned away, as I always did, too caught up in the storm of my thoughts to pay them any mind.

Somewhere in the background of all this, I had missed noticing someone—someone who seemed to know something but chose to stay silent. Was it fear that held them back? Or just indifference? I couldn't tell. They had been a quiet observer of the unfolding events, lingering on the edge of my awareness like a shadow I couldn't shake.

As I drove on, weaving through the city's endless pulse of life, I began to feel it—the sense of being watched. Unseen eyes seemed to track my every move. The memory of that silent figure who knew more than they let on clung to me, gnawing at the edges of my thoughts. Would I ever see them again? It felt unlikely, yet their motives—or lack of them—left me restless, and uneasy.

Even as the city hummed and surged, I couldn't rid myself of the sense that this silent spectator would return, in a way I couldn't predict. There was something inevitable about it like a storm waiting to break. Every passing moment deepened the feeling that their quiet presence would soon shift the course of my life—and the lives of others tied to me. The suspense of the unknown hung heavy, filling me with a mix of anticipation and dread for whatever twist lay ahead.

The Present

Chapter 15

As I stood at the altar, waiting for Shayna to walk down the aisle, my mind drifted back to the night we first met at the Embassy party. It had been a whirlwind of an evening, filled with laughter, sparkling conversation, and the thrill of meeting someone who seemed to understand me in a way no one else ever had.

And now, as she made her way towards me, her eyes sparkling with love and excitement, I couldn't help but feel a surge of gratitude for the twist of fate that had brought us together.

We to each other, promising to navigate the challenges of a long-distance relationship with patience, trust, and unwavering support. We remained in touch as she left to pursue her academic journey. We embraced technology as our lifeline, using phone calls, video chats, and countless text messages to bridge the gap between us.

There were moments of loneliness and longing when the ache of missing each other felt almost unbearable. But in those moments, we drew strength from the love that bound us together, finding solace in the knowledge that our separation was only temporary.

We each other whenever possible, cherishing the precious moments we spent together and creating memories to sustain us during the times apart. Whether it was a quick getaway as I combined my official trips to the US to add a week to meet with her or a spontaneous road trip, each reunion was a celebration of our love and a reminder of the depth of our connection.

As our relationship deepened unsure of how Shayna would react to hearing about my previous dalliances. But to my surprise, she listened with an open heart and a non-judgmental ea

"I know we all have a past," she said softly, her eyes meeting mine with unwavering sincerity. "What matters is who we are now and where we are headed. And with you, I see a future filled with love, trust, and mutual respect."

Her words washed over me, soothing the doubts and insecurities that had plagued me for so long. In Shayna, I found not only acceptance but also forgiveness—a willingness to look past my mistakes and see the person I had become, flaws and all.

One evening, as we sat together in her living room, the topic organically, prompted by a passing mention of her family's wealth. I hesitated at first, unsure of how to broach the subject, but Shayna sensed my unease and gently encouraged me to share my thoughts.

"I can't help but feel a bit intimidated sometimes," I admitted, my voice tinged with vulnerability. "Your family's wealth—it's like a whole other world to me. I worry that I won't be able to measure up, that I won't be able to provide for you in the way they can."

Shayna listened quietly, her expression soft and understanding. "I understand where you're coming from," she said gently, reaching out to take my hand in hers. "But you have to know that money has never mattered to me as much as love and compatibility do. What matters most is that we are happy together, that we support each other through thick and thin."

Her words filled me with a sense of relief as if a weight had been lifted from my shoulders. "I just don't want to feel like I'm holding you back," I confessed, my voice barely above a whisper.

"You could never hold me back," Shayna replied firmly, her eyes locking with mine. "We're in this together, as equals. And if anyone has a problem with that, then they don't understand what true love is."

At that moment, I realized just how lucky I was to have Shayna by my side—to have someone who valued me not for what I could provide materially, but for the person I was inside. With her understanding, I knew that we could overcome any obstacle, including the economic disparity between us and her parents. As we held each other close, I felt a renewed sense of confidence in our love and our future together.

We supported each other through the ups and downs of life, cheering each other on from afar as we pursued our dreams and chased our goals. We celebrated each other's successes, her graduation, and my promotion and offered comfort in times of disappointment, knowing that no matter what obstacles we faced, we were stronger together.

As we stood amidst the throngs of proud graduates and their families, the excitement in the air was palpable. Shayna had just graduated from Wharton, a momentous achievement that marked the culmination of years of hard work and dedication. To top it off, she had been offered a position at a major private equity firm in India where she wanted to return to—a dream come true for her and a source of immense pride for me.

As we made our way through the crowd, Shayna's face lit up with a radiant smile, her eyes sparkling with joy and anticipation. I couldn't help but feel a swell of pride in my chest, knowing that she had worked tirelessly to reach this moment, and that her efforts had finally paid off in spectacular fashion.

"Congratulations, Shayna," I said, unable to contain my excitement. "I'm so incredibly proud of you. Graduating from Wharton and landing a job at a top private equity firm— it's truly an amazing accomplishment."

Shayna beamed at me, her cheeks flushed with happiness. "Thank you," she said, her voice filled with emotion. "I couldn't have done it without your love and support. Youve been my rock throughout this journey, and I'm so grateful to have you by my side."

I pulled her into a tight embrace, savoring the moment as we basked in the glow of her success. "I will always be here for you, Shayna," I whispered, pressing a kiss to her forehead. "I believe in you, and I know that you're going to do incredible things in your career."

Shayna rested her head against my chest, her arms wrapped around me in a gesture of gratitude and affection. "I love you," she murmured, her words a sweet melody that echoed in my heart.

"I love you too," I replied, holding her close as we stood together, united in our love and our shared dreams for the future. In that moment, surrounded by the promise of new beginnings and endless possibilities, I knew that our love was stronger than ever, and that together, we could conquer the world.

And as the days turned into weeks, weeks into months and the months to years, we grew even closer, our love deepening with each passing day. We learned to cherish the moments we shared, to savor the small joys of life, and to never take each other for granted.

Eventually, the distance between us began to fade away, replaced by a profound sense of closeness and intimacy that transcended physical boundaries. And when the time finally came for us to be together again, it felt like coming home—to each other, and to the love that had sustained us through it all.

The day had been meticulously planned, every detail carefully orchestrated to create the perfect moment for the most important question of my life. With the ring safely tucked away in my pocket and a nervous excitement coursing through my veins, I set out to make Shayna's dreams and mine come true.

I knew Shayna had always dreamed of visiting the botanical gardens, a place where she could lose herself in the beauty of nature and find solace amidst the chaos of everyday life. It seemed like the ideal setting for what I had in mind—a serene oasis where I could declare my love for her beneath the canopy of blooming flowers and swaying trees.

As we strolled hand in hand through the winding pathways of the garden, Shayna's laughter filled the air, her eyes sparkling with joy and wonder. I couldn't help but smile, knowing that soon I would be the one to bring tears of happiness to her eyes.

We found ourselves in a secluded corner of the garden, a tranquil spot overlooking a shimmering pond dotted with lily pads. The soft light of the setting sun cast a warm glow over the scene, bathing everything in a golden hue.

Taking a deep breath to steady my nerves, I turned to face Shayna, my heart pounding in my chest. With trembling hands, I reached into my pocket and retrieved the ring, its sparkle catching the light as if it were alive with anticipation.

Words failed me in that moment, so instead, I let my actions speak for themselves. Dropping to one knee, I took Shayna's hand in mine, my eyes locked with hers as I poured out my heart in a rush of emotion.

"Shayna," I began, my voice barely above a whisper, "from the moment et you, I knew you were the one. You are my best friend, my confidante, and my soulmate. I cannot imagine my life without you in it, and I don't want to. Will you do me the honor of spending the rest of your life with me?"

Tears had welled up in Shayna's eyes as she looked down at me, her hand covering her mouth in disbelief. For a moment, time seemed to stand still as we savored the magic of the moment, the world fading away until there was only the two of us, bound together by love.

And then, with a joyous cry, Shayna threw her arms around me, her answer clear before she even spoke a word. "Yes," she whispered, her voice filled with emotion. "A thousand times, yes."

In that moment, surrounded by the beauty of nature and the warmth of our love, I knew that my proposal had been everything Shayna had ever dreamed of—and so much more. And as we sealed our love with a kiss, I couldn't help but feel grateful for the chance to spend the rest of my life with the woman of my dreams.

Our wedding day had finally arrived, a day filled with laughter, tears of joy, and the promise of a lifetime spent in each other's embrace.

As Shayna reached my side, her hand slipped into mine, fitting perfectly as if it had always belonged there. With tears of joy in our eyes, we exchanged vows, promising to love and cherish one another for all eternity.

As the sun dipped below the horizon, casting a warm golden hue over the landscape, we stood hand in hand, ready to embark on a journey together—a journey of love, companionship, and shared dreams.

Surrounded by our closest friends and family, we exchanged vows beneath a canopy of flowers, pledging our love and devotion to one another in front of all who mattered most to us.

The air was alive with excitement and anticipation as we danced beneath the twinkling lights, our hearts overflowing with happiness and gratitude for the love that had brought us together. With each step we took on the dance floor, we wove a tapestry of memories that would last a lifetime—a testament to the bond we shared and the adventures that lay ahead.

As the night wore on and the festivities continued, we stole quiet moments together, savoring the sweetness of our newfound union. With every glance, every touch, we reaffirmed our commitment to one another, cherishing the love that had blossomed between us.

As the evening drew to a close, we found ourselves bathed in the soft glow of candlelight, our hearts full to bursting with love and gratitude for the blessings that had brought us together. Hand in hand, we stepped into the future, ready to face whatever challenges may come our way, secure in the knowledge that as long as we had each other, we could weather any storm.

As we sealed our union with a kiss, I knew that no matter what the future held, as long as I had Shayna by my side, I would always be home.

Chapter 16

The first casualty of our marriage was the house we lived in. It was too small especially considering the affluent background that Shayna came from. Although she never expressed it, I felt it in my hear that she would definitely have preferred a larger house.

I started looking for a place in Gurgaon which would be closer to my workplace as also hers. The apartments were larger at a much lower cost as compared to Delhi, so it was just the mix I needed to make a final decision and give Shayna what she deserved. The clincher came when her parents offered to gift us the apartment in Gurgaon. My initial reaction was to politely decline but the look on Shayna's face forced me to relent and accept the offer

The house I had called home for so long seemed to hold its breath as I packed the last of my belongings. Each room, once brimming with life and familiarity, now stood hollow.

I confidently declared to our Bihari landlord, "Uncle, we've decided to move out of this house."

He responded with a resounding burp, fumbling for a cloth to wipe his mouth before turning his attention to me.

"Where are you going?" he asked, his curiosity evident.

I marveled at the thought that we had spent so many years in this same rented accommodation. "How time flies," I mused internally before sharing with excitement, "I've bought a house for myself in DLF, Gurgaon."

His reaction was swift. "How big is it?"

"Four-bedrooms," I announced, the pride in my voice unmistakable. His astonishment was palpable. I could almost see the mental calculations in his head—perhaps he regretted not charging us more rent all these years.

"Good. When I was your age, I was just as focused as you are. You've done well for yourself. You came here just after your marriage, and now, after five years, you're moving into your own house. Very good," he said, a faint glimmer of pride softening his usual stern demeanour.

Over the years, I had come to view him differently—a father figure in some ways. Now, as we discussed my departure, that fatherly warmth seemed to wane.

"Achcha, so when do you plan to vacate? Remember, you have to give me one month's notice," he reminded me with his business-like tone.

"So much for the father-son equation," I thought to myself. Aloud, I said, "I'd like to move in 15 days."

He hesitated but eventually relented. "Alright...pay me 15 days' rent. And... you must come visit us once you're settled in DLF," he added, a touch of wistfulness creeping into his voice.

I thanked him and turned towards the stairs. As I glanced back, I caught a fleeting image of the man behind the gruff exterior—a vulnerable figure, his emotions laid bare as he wiped a tear and retreated into his bedroom.

With all the formalities completed, Shayna and I settled into a beautiful apartment in The Aralias in DLF. Her lucrative job with a private equity firm, my steady rise at a major IT company, and a generous contribution from her family made the fancy apartment within reach.

Every day, I grew more attuned to the subtle contrasts between Delhi and the so-called National Capital Region. DLF had much more to offer than just liquor stores. The cost of living was higher, and the neighborhood was populated mostly by executives from multinational corporations.

The high-rises, with their 24-hour power backup, water supply, and robust security, were a godsend. Life here had a charm of its own, and I was beginning to savor it. However, beneath the surface of this seemingly smooth transition, a quiet tension brewed. Unbeknownst to me, this move would trigger a series of events that would shatter the calm of my newfound life in DLF.

DLF was supposed to be a fresh start, a blank canvas for my new life after marriage. Everyone said it was a dream, yet a strange unease followed me.

The new house was beautiful, yes, but its perfection felt sterile, almost too polished to be real. I couldn't shake the feeling that I'd left more behind than a house.

The storm that was coming would rattle the foundations of everything I thought I knew about my life, my choices, and myself.

Chapter 17

Shayna and I have experienced countless moments of joy, laughter, and love in our lives since getting married. It was hard to believe that a year had already passed since we'd embarked on this journey together. In that time, our bond had grown stronger and deeper with every passing day.

Together, we'd weathered storms and celebrated victories, supporting one another through the highs and lows of life with unwavering love and commitment. From lazy Sunday mornings spent in each other's arms to late-night conversations that stretched into the early hours, every moment with Shayna had been a treasure—a precious gift I held close to my heart.

We'd explored new places, tried new things, and discovered hidden depths within ourselves and each other. Through it all, Shayna had been my partner, my confidante, and my best friend—a constant source of strength and inspiration in a world that could often feel uncertain and chaotic.

Together, we'd faced challenges head-on, finding solace in the knowledge that we were stronger together than we could ever be apart. As we navigated life's ups and downs, our love only deepened, anchoring us in a sea of uncertainty and guiding us toward a future filled with hope and possibility.

The birth of our daughter brought indescribable joy and an overwhelming sense of gratitude. From the first moment we held her in our arms, we knew our lives would never be the same again—that this tiny, precious bundle of joy was the greatest gift we could ever receive.

As we gazed into her eyes for the first time, our hearts swelled with love and wonder, marveling at the miracle of her existence. She was perfect in every way, a tiny reflection of the love we shared—a love that had created life itself.

In the days and weeks that followed, we marveled at the wonder of parenthood, navigating sleepless nights and endless nappy changes with a mixture of awe and exhaustion. Every coo, every smile, every milestone became a celebration—a testament to the incredible journey that lay ahead of us as a family.

Together, we watched our daughter grow and flourish, her laughter filling our home with warmth and light. We reveled in the simple joys of parenthood—snuggles on the couch, tickle fights before bedtime, and lazy afternoons in the park.

In her, we saw the promise of a future brimming with endless possibilities—a future we would navigate hand in hand, as a family. As I looked to the road ahead, I felt a sense of excitement and anticipation, knowing that whatever challenges might come, we'd face them together, just as we always had.

"Let's go to a movie tonight," Shayna exclaimed, breaking the calm of the evening.

"Which one?" I asked, setting my book aside.

"Bajrangi Bhaijaan—it's the only option we have," she said, scrolling through her iPad with quick flicks of her finger.

"Alright," I agreed. "And how do we manage our daughter?"

"My mum can take care of her. It's a 10:40 pm show, and she'll be fast asleep by then anyway," came Shayna's ready reply.

It sounded logical, so off we went.

The movie, unfortunately, was passable at best and dragged on far too long for my liking. Shayna, on the other hand, seemed to love it purely because Salman Khan was in it. The story and acting were minor details she happily overlooked as long as he graced the screen.

The subterranean parking lot was a kaleidoscope of cars, each more opulent than the last.

We drove home in near silence. Shayna crashed as soon as we arrived, while I decided to pour myself a drink. It was already past 1:45 am.

As I aimlessly flicked through TV channels, an image flashed in my mind—Jannat from GB Road. I couldn't pinpoint what had triggered the memory; perhaps it was the little girl's presence in the movie. The thought lingered, unrelated yet insistent. It had been nearly seven years since our first meeting and over a year since our last, but the memories were as vivid as if had all happened yesterday.

An urgency stirred within me, and the plan I'd been harboring demanded action. On instinct, I dialed Manoj's number.

The phone rang for a while before he answered, his voice heavy with sleep.

"Arre yaar, remember Jannat?" I blurted out.

"Jannat who?" he asked groggily.

"The girl we met at GB Road," I said, hoping to jog his memory.

"Did you fucking call me at this hour to ask about her? Are you crazy? What about her? Don't tell me you're missing her. She'll be busy now," he said, letting out a laugh despite his drowsy state.

"No," I replied, my tone firm. "I want to meet her one more time. Will you come with me?"

"Are you bloody mad? We swore never to go back there!" His voice grew sharper. "What's the point of this, Dinesh? Now and then, you get these guilt pangs, call me, and then we go there, only for you to forget about her again. It's a cycle. What's different this time?"

"You're right, but I need closure," I admitted. "I have a plan. I'll explain everything when we meet. If you don't want to come, I'll go alone."

Manoj sighed, his initial anger giving way to reluctant curiosity. "When do you want to go?"

"Can we go tonight?" I asked, uncertain.

"It's nearly 2 am, man. Not a good idea. Let's go tomorrow morning, same time as before. It's a weekend."

"Thanks, Manoj." I heard the line go dead.

That night, I couldn't sleep. Tossing and turning, I wrestled with my thoughts. Manoj was right—why did I keep returning to this? A memory would resurface, guilt would follow, and I'd act on impulse. This time, I vowed, would be different. The plan I'd crafted in my head would finally come to fruition.

As sleep overtook me, her last words echoed faintly in my mind. What were they? I struggled to remember.

I knew I needed someone besides Manoj to make my plan work, and it had to be her. She could help, but her motives were shrouded in mystery. Would she be an ally or a complication? The question loomed as I drifted into an uneasy slumber.

The bigger question was this: My plan needed help to execute and I was not sure whom I could turn to. A name kept popping up. I knew she would not trust me but a larger question loomed in my head. Could I trust her?

Chapter 18

Formed a peculiar tradition of sorts with our visits to G.B. Road—the infamous red-light district of Delhi. Though we referred to these outings as "pilgrimages" with a hint of irony, there was an unspoken camaraderie in our shared ventures, a bond forged through friendship and mutual understanding.

Hailing an auto-rickshaw, we set off. The bustling energy of Connaught Place slowly gave way to quieter anticipation as the chaos faded into the background. Something about G.B. Road always called me back—a chaotic energy, a shroud of mystery, and an allure I couldn't quite shake.

Arriving at our destination, the dusty streets and cacophony of G.B. Road enveloped us. It was a place seemingly untouched by time, where the past and present collided in uneasy harmony. The labyrinthine alleyways and the clatter of life here were a stark reminder of the city's darker realities.

"Right, what's this plan of yours?" Manoj asked, breaking the spell.

I pulled a small flip phone from my pocket. "I'm giving this to her. She can use it to let me know when she visits the paanwallah next. Indrani and someone from the Social Welfare Cell will join us then."

"So, Indrani finally answered your call?" Manoj teased, grinning.

I kept my tone steady. "She did. Now, we'll need Jannat's cooperation. The phone will let us bypass her pimps, so we don't have to go through this circus every time."

"Why not just send the Welfare Cell to raid the place and rescue her?" Manoj asked, skepticism creeping into his voice.

"That won't work. These guys have everything set up legally—or so it seems. Even if there's a raid, the girls are too scared to say anything. They'd back their maalkin out of fear. If Jannat agrees to leave willingly, no one can accuse us of kidnapping. That's our only shot."

Manoj nodded slowly, though I could tell he wasn't entirely convinced.

"This might work," he said after a pause. "But it's risky. What if they find the phone on her? And even if she said she wanted out, there's no guarantee she'll still feel the same."

"That's a risk I'm willing to take," I replied firmly. "The paanwallah confirmed she steps out occasionally. We'll time it. If not, we'll agree on a date and wait for her. It's a gamble, but if it works, we'll have done something good."

Manoj sighed, the weight of the plan sinking in. "Alright. We don't have much to lose. Let's do it."

We hailed another auto-rickshaw, navigating the strange protocol of requesting, not directing, a Delhi auto driver.

"Which kotha?" the driver asked knowingly.

Déjà vu hit me hard. The same sights, smells, and sounds from a year ago overwhelmed my senses. I scanned the alleys for familiar landmarks, searching for the staircase that had once led us to Jannat.

"Come this way," Manoj said, reading my thoughts.

He moved with ease; the map of this place etched into his memory. Minutes later, we stood before a familiar staircase flanked by hardware shops. A shopkeeper glanced at us, recognition flickering across his face or so I thought.

"We'll have to take our chances," Manoj murmured, leading the way up.

At the top, a burly, dark-skinned man stopped us, suspicion etched into his expression.

"Where are you going?" he barked.

"We're looking for Jannat," I said before I could stop myself.

Manoj shot me a glare but quickly recovered. "We were here a while back," he said smoothly. "Had a great time with a girl named Jannat. Delighted us both. We'd like her again but for the whole day this time."

The man's stance relaxed slightly. "There were two girls named Jannat," he replied. "One died of TB. The other's still around, I think. Her name's real, not one she made up for clients. Maybe she's the one you're after."

The words hit me like a blow. Two Jannats. One gone. Was the one who had died the girl we sought?

"Can you take us to her?" I asked, trying to keep my voice steady.

"For 5,000 rupees," he said, his tone blunt. "You want her, you pay."

"That's too much," Manoj countered.

"Fine. Then get lost." The man turned to leave.

"Wait!" I said, pulling out a wad of notes. "We have 3,000. Please, take it."

The man's eyes gleamed. He snatched the money and gestured for us to follow.

The corridors grew darker and narrower as we walked. Finally, we stopped outside a room, its entrance covered by a tattered curtain.

"Go on," the man said. "I'll wait here. Let me know what you want."

Manoj pushed the curtain aside. A girl sat on the bed, her expression a mixture of fear and weariness.

For a moment, hope surged within me—but it was extinguished almost immediately. She wasn't Jannat.

The weight of disappointment settled on us. The girl wasn't who we'd been searching for. The shadow of failure loomed large, but we couldn't stop now.

"This isn't over," I whispered to Manoj.

"No," he agreed. "But we'll need to try harder."

The quest for Jannat wasn't just about finding her—it was about confronting the harsh truths of this world and though we left empty-handed that day, determination burned brighter than ever.

Chapter 19

"What the heck?"

"She's not the one?" asked the pimp, his tone indifferent.

"No, she's not," I replied, the disappointment palpable.

"A thousand Jannats come and go every year," he said with a shrug. "It's impossible to keep track. Some of them move on to bigger things."

The room seemed to close on us, the harsh reality settling like a bitter weight. The pimp's callous words lingered in the air, a grim reminder of the transient and brutal lives that passed through the dimly lit corridors of G.B. Road.

"Shit," I muttered, unsure what else to say. "What now?"

"If you like, we've got some fresh stock. Will that work?" he asked, his crass suggestion igniting a flash of anger in me.

I clenched my fists, ready to lash out, but Manoj caught my eye and shook his head. He stepped forward, his voice calm and measured. "Sirjee, we were just enquiring. We wouldn't mind another, but that one was special."

The pimp softened slightly. "Business is slow these days. I'd like to help you out. But first, level with me. You're not cops or some NGO types, right? No social welfare bullshit?"

Manoj and I exchanged a glance before shaking our heads emphatically. "No, we're not," Manoj assured him.

"A year is a long time," the pimp said, his tone growing conspiratorial. "I can't help you, but I can take you to someone who might know. It'll cost you. She's an old-timer—past her prime—but for the right price, she won't mind snitching. Nobody goes to her kotha anymore, so she'll welcome the money."

Desperation outweighed caution, and we negotiated a hefty fee. After some haggling, the pimp agreed to lead us to a woman named Neerja bi. The journey through the narrow corridors felt suffocating, each step echoing with the weight of the lives lived and lost there.

"Neerja bi!" the pimp called out as we entered a dimly lit room. "Someone's here to ask you something."

Perched on a worn couch, an elderly woman was chewing paan, her weathered face betraying a mix of suspicion and apathy. She eyed us warily as the pimp whispered something in her ear.

"So, you're looking for a girl?" she said, her voice sharp and distrustful. "Why her in particular? There are plenty here who can meet your needs."

Manoj laughed, trying to ease the tension. "We can look at others, but we'd prefer her," he said, the humor in his voice cutting through the heavy air.

"Are you talking about the one with thick, jet-black hair?" she asked, her suspicion beginning to thaw.

I nodded, memories of Jannat rushing back, but before I could respond, she interrupted. "I don't trust you," she said bluntly. She turned to the pimp. "Have you checked these guys? Cameras? Mics? Are they from some social service department?"

"They're clean, Neerja bi," the pimp lied smoothly.

Her eyes narrowed before she relented. "I do remember a girl like that. Was she the one with a scar on her leg?"

My heart raced. "Yes, that's her," I said, unable to hide my excitement.

The scar. I remembered the story behind it, a harrowing tale Jannat had shared with us—a reminder of the horrors she'd endured.

"That scar," Neerja bi began, her voice heavy with the weight of the past, "was no accident. A corrupt cop did that to her. She never talked much about it, but we all knew."

The room felt stifling as she recounted the details. The scar wasn't just a mark—it was a testament to Jannat's resilience and strength, carved into her flesh by cruelty but worn as a badge of survival.

"She was different," Neerja bi continued. "Had dreams of being a doctor, if you can believe it. Seven years here, and she never gave up hope. Stupid girl."

"That sounds like her," I thought, the past tense in her words twisting my stomach.

"She's not here anymore," she said, almost apologetically. "She was sold a few months ago. Someone paid good money for her, and we haven't seen her since. New girls come in all the time, and the old ones have to make way."

The revelation hit me like a sledgehammer. The hope I'd clung to felt like it was slipping through my fingers.

"Do you know who bought her?" Manoj asked hesitantly.

Neerja bi's expression hardened. "Even if I knew, I wouldn't tell you. This isn't your world, boys. Go home. Forget her. This place will chew you up and spit you out. Sabhi ek doosre ko choona laga rahein hai yahaan. (Everyone here is out to screw someone else.)"

The pimp stepped forward, his eyes gleaming with greed. "If you need anything else, let me know," he said, motioning us toward the exit.

We descended the stairs in silence, each step heavier than the last. At the bottom, I turned to Manoj.

"Now what?" I asked, my voice hollow.

"Forget it, Dinesh," he said firmly. "This is a dead end. Let it go before we get ourselves killed."

But something about Neerja bi's parting words nagged at me. "Take the paan from Sadiq Ali," she'd said with a cryptic smile.

"The paanwallah," I whispered, the realization hitting me.

"What?" Manoj asked, confused.

"Sadiq Ali Paan Corner—the guy we talked to last year. Maybe he knows something."

Manoj stared at me for a moment, then sighed. "Alright. Let's go."

We retraced our steps through the labyrinthine streets, determination propelling us forward. The sign for Sadiq Ali Paan Corner gleamed in the dim light, a beacon of hope in the chaos.

"Kya lenge, Saab?" the paanwallah greeted us, his twirly mustache as vibrant as I remembered.

"Do you remember us?" I asked, trying to gauge his reaction.

He squinted at us, then shook his head. "Maybe, maybe not. I'm getting old."

"Do you remember Jannat?" I asked, my voice steady despite the turmoil within.

At the mention of her name, he froze, his expression betraying a flicker of recognition.

In that suspended moment, hope ignited anew.

Chapter 20

The paan shop held a revelation that reignited our quest. As we confronted Sadiq Ali, the paanwallah, a flicker of recognition crossed his face. The young boy from our previous visit, now slightly taller, silently observed us, his gaze unwavering as if recognizing our persistence.

It felt like an eternity before Sadiq Ali finally spoke. "Oh, my God," he exclaimed, his voice tinged with surprise. "You're the same guys who came here a few years ago. I remember you. You were the ones who asked about Jannat—not like the hundred others who ask with very different intentions. Nobody cares about anyone here, but you… you seemed different. Yes, yes, it's all coming back to me now."

The boy, still cleaning the shelves, continued to maintain eye contact, his actions deliberate and measured. He stacked some bills on the counter, but Manoj caught sight of him tearing one and slipping it into his pocket before disappearing to the back of the shop.

Hope surged within me. Another breakthrough at last. Manoj, catching my eye, smiled faintly. "Does she still visit you?" he asked.

Sadiq Ali's expression grew somber as he glanced around cautiously. "Have you asked anyone else? I saw you coming from that direction," he said, motioning toward the kotha we'd just left.

"Yes," I replied, hesitating. "We met a—"

"A pimp," Manoj interjected smoothly. "He took our money and led us to another Jannat, but she wasn't the one. Nobody seems to know where she is."

The paanwallah nodded knowingly. "That's true. Nobody knows. She left shortly after your last visit. I would've forgotten her too, but… her innocence—stayed with me. It's not something you can easily ignore."

"She left?" I repeated, disbelief creeping into my voice. "But I thought leaving wasn't an option here."

Sadiq Ali sighed deeply. "She used to come here for paan or cigarettes, sometimes for Neerja bi, sometimes just to talk. She confided in me, like a daughter talking to a father. Once, she mentioned that Neerja Bi was planning to sell her. I believed her because that's how it works here. She was probably sold to someone for a good sum. Morality doesn't exist in this place, Saab."

I debated whether to mention that Neerja bi had subtly directed us here but decided against it. We might have misread her intentions, and I didn't want to plant false hope in this fragile situation.

"Some girls are eventually sold off when they've outlived their utility," Sadiq Ali continued. "I tried to forget her—helps numb the pain. I'd started seeing her as a daughter, you see. So, you can understand how it hurt to lose her."

"Do you know where she went?" I asked, clinging to a shred of hope.

Sadiq Ali shook his head, resignation evident in his voice. "I don't know. She left shortly after you came last time. Maybe she's dead now. Who knows in this place?"

As he served other customers, Sadiq Ali called out to the boy. "Arre Chottu! Get that box out of the way, you fool. How long have you been here and still can't figure out what needs to be done? Idiot!"

Chottu emerged from the back, embarrassed and fearful, scurrying to move the boxes. Sadiq Ali turned back to us; his voice tinged with the indifference born of time. "Would you like a cigarette?"

"I'll have a Marlboro Light," I replied.

"Oye, Chottu! Marlboro Light for Saab!" Sadiq Ali shouted.

As I lit my cigarette, I noticed a commotion outside one of the kothas. The paanwallah stepped out to investigate, leaving Chottu to hand me the cigarette. The boy's wide-eyed gaze stayed fixed on me and Manoj as though he wanted to say something but couldn't.

Sadiq Ali returned, chuckling. "Same old story, a customer getting beaten up for not paying. Happens every day."

Glancing toward the commotion, I saw the burly man from earlier emerge for a smoke. If he spotted us lingering, it wouldn't be long before his suspicions were aroused.

I quickly handed Sadiq Ali a crumpled ten-rupee note. "Thank you," I said, disappointment heavy in my voice. Manoj and I turned to leave.

The paanwallah pocketed the money indifferently, shifting his focus to the next customer as the chaos of the street resumed around him.

As we walked away, Manoj voiced what I was thinking. "That wasn't very useful," he said, his tone resigned.

I nodded. "Maybe Neerja bi wasn't giving us a clue after all. Maybe we got our hopes up for nothing."

Manoj sighed. "Yeah. Let's just grab a rickshaw and get out of here."

We spotted one at the corner of the street, its driver stubbing out a beedi before wiping his face with his vest. As we approached, I felt a tap on my shoulder.

Turning, I saw Chottu standing there, his small frame barely noticeable amidst the crowd. In his hand was my mobile phone, which I'd left behind at the shop.

"Oh, thank God! Thank you, Chottu," I said, relief washing over me.

As I reached for the phone, Chottu held my hand firmly and slipped a small, folded piece of paper under it. His eyes darted nervously around before he let go, his urgency silencing my questions.

I tucked the paper away discreetly, exchanging a glance with Manoj, who seemed equally puzzled.

Back in the rickshaw, I unfolded the note. Scrawled in hurried, barely legible writing were the words:

B 16/22, Khirki.

"What does that even mean?" Manoj asked, peering over my shoulder.

"It looks like an address," I replied, my mind racing. "But why would he give this to us?"

"Maybe it's a clue," Manoj suggested. "Or a mistake."

"No," I said firmly. "He didn't want us to open it near the paanwallah. He knew exactly what he was doing."

Manoj studied the note again. "Alright, let's check it out. What have we got to lose?"

As the rickshaw rattled along the city's uneven streets, the cryptic note in my hand became our guiding thread. Despite the setbacks, a renewed sense of purpose pushed us forward. The search for Jannat wasn't over—not yet.

Chapter 21

"Aman, where are you? Stop playing games. Where are you?"

"He's probably sleeping somewhere to shirk work," muttered the man as he turned a page of his newspaper. It was his day off—the day both Nilofer and Aman dreaded. A day spent enduring a man devoid of sensitivity, someone who treated everyone around him as less than human.

"He must be outside cleaning the car, Abba," Nilofer offered, trying to defuse the tension.

Outside, Aman resumed cleaning the car, the rhythmic scrubbing offering a small reprieve from the heavy silence that hung over the household. Nilofer, having borne her father's harsh words countless times, felt a familiar mix of frustration and resignation. She knew the truth behind his cruelty and despised the compromises she had to make to keep peace.

The man remained engrossed in his newspaper, seemingly oblivious to the emotional turmoil he sowed. Aman, on the other hand, silently shouldered his burdens, his weariness etched into his young face.

Nilofer broke the uneasy silence. "Abba, it's your day off, but we all have responsibilities. Aman is working hard and always tries to help you. Let's not ruin the day with unnecessary arguments."

Her words earned only a dismissive grunt. The strained relationship between them hung like a storm cloud. Nilofer exchanged a glance with Aman, a silent acknowledgment of their shared struggles.

The man barked from his seat, "Get me a cup of tea, you lazy idiot!"

Aman paused, the insult sinking in, but he said nothing. The fragile equilibrium of the household was one he had long grown accustomed to navigating.

The man repeated himself, this time to Nilofer. "Tell that idiot to bring me tea. He can't talk, but at least he can make tea."

"Yes, Abba," Nilofer replied quietly as she stepped outside to find Aman. "There you are," she said, spotting him. "Abba's calling for tea. You'd better hurry." She nudged him gently, her voice soft but urgent.

Aman dropped the rag, washed his hands at the outdoor tap, and followed her inside.

"There you are, you good-for-nothing!" the man barked. "Nilofer, you've spoiled him too much, protecting him all the time. Let him fend for himself. He needs to learn!"

"Abba, he works 16 to 18 hours a day and he is only a child. He barely has time for himself," Nilofer countered. "I'm teaching him English and Maths. He's learning quickly."

"What good will that do? The boy's dim-witted. The only reason I brought him home was to work—help around the house and at the shop. He gets food and shelter in return. That's more than enough!"

Nilofer swallowed the retort forming in her mind. She wanted to shout, What about his self-respect, Abba? But knew it was pointless.

"The only reason I tolerate him is because he keeps you company. You treat him like the little brother you never had, and I don't want to ruin that."

Aman returned with tea on a tray, placing it before the man, who sipped and grunted approvingly. "The only thing he's good for is making tea. Now get back to the car!"

"You always do this, Abba," Nilofer said, her voice tinged with sadness.

The man turned to her, narrowing his eyes. "Do what?"

"You let people go. Just like my sister. It's only a matter of time before you do the same with him, isn't it?"

"That's an old story," her father snapped. "I wish you'd put it behind you. I did what I had to."

"No, Abba. You did what was convenient. You behaved like a coward."

"Stop it, Nilofer!" he shouted, anger flashing in his eyes. "How dare you speak to me like that! After all, I've done for you, this is how you repay me? You ungrateful wretch!"

Nilofer lowered her head, knowing any argument was futile. It was like talking to a brick wall. A part of her despised him enough to wish him gone, but the fear of an uncertain future kept her tethered to this life.

She gestured to Aman to return to the car. He silently obeyed, picking up the rag and bucket of water. But as he resumed cleaning, a thought had begun to fester in his mind—a thought that now demanded action.

"It won't be long," he murmured to himself.

Nilofer stepped outside, the tension inside the house suffocating her. She approached Aman. "Don't let what Abba says upset you. He doesn't mean it."

"Didi, I saying," Aman said, his voice tentative.

"Oh? What is it?" Nilofer asked, her tone softening as she cupped his face with her hands.

"I think… right I do," Aman stammered.

Nilofer's brow furrowed. "What do you mean, Aman? Did you… oh my God." Her eyes widened. "Aman, did you do something to Abba's tea?"

Aman grabbed her hand, pulling her behind the car. "Nu… nu," he whispered urgently, his face a mixture of fear and resolve.

"What is it, Aman? Tell me!" she pleaded.

He paused, struggling to find the words, his lips moving silently as if rehearsing each one. It took him a while, but slowly, haltingly, he began to recount the events of the previous day, his voice breaking the silence in uneven, cautious fragments.

Nilofer listened in stunned silence, her heart sinking as the weight of his actions became clear. When he finished, she pulled him into a tight embrace.

"Aman, why? Why did you do that? We're all in trouble now. What are we going to do?" Her voice trembled, her mind racing through the potential consequences.

In the dim alley behind the car, Aman's regret was palpable. He had acted impulsively, driven by a desperate need to protect Nilofer, but now, confronted with the reality of his actions, doubt gnawed at him.

"We'll figure something out," Nilofer whispered, trying to steady her voice. "We always do."

Yet, even as she spoke, the uncertainty of their precarious lives loomed large. One wrong move could bring everything crashing down.

Their bond, tested like never before, held firm in the shadow of their shared fear. For now, they had each other and that would have to be enough.

Chapter 22

The morning carried a sense of unusual weight. I was lounging in bed, unsure of how to start my day, when Shayna walked in holding a crumpled piece of paper.

"Do you need this?" she asked, her tone neutral. "The maid found it in your jeans pocket before throwing them into the washing machine."

I took the slip from her hand and read the scribbled note:

B 16/22 Khirki

The events of the previous day surged back in vivid detail. "I don't know," I murmured, lost in thought. I began recounting the day's events to Shayna, who started mildly disinterested but gradually sat down, her attention hooked as the story unfolded.

"So, that's what this is all about. I have no idea what to make of it. What do you think?" I asked, hoping she'd provide clarity on where Manoj and I had failed.

"It's an address," she said thoughtfully. "Khirki Village, near Malviya Nagar, maybe? Remember when we used to..."

"Oh my God," I interrupted, realization dawning. "Yes, Khirki village! How could I have missed that? I lived in Malviya Nagar for years!"

"Who do you know in Khirki village?" she asked incredulously as she walked back into the other room.

The paper felt heavier in my hand now, its mysterious significance amplifying the unease it brought. Chottu's furtive demeanor when he handed it to me lingered in my mind, adding layers of complexity to the puzzle.

I couldn't shake the barrage of questions. Why had Chottu given me this? What was its connection to Jannat? Could this be a lead, or was it a dead end? The uncertainty clouded my thoughts.

The city outside buzzed with its usual chaos, oblivious to the storm of confusion in my mind. Clutching the note, I felt the weight of responsibility and the urgency of our search pressing on me. "Should I head to the address now or wait to gather more information?" The indecision gnawed at me, a labyrinth of questions without answers.

I instinctively reached for my phone and dialed Manoj.

"Hey, Manoj."

"Hi, man. What's up? I was meaning to call you. Something's been bothering me since yesterday."

"Is it about the note?" I asked.

"Yeah. I've been thinking—"

"Hold that thought. The address is in Khirki, near Malviya Nagar," I interjected.

"Hmm, so we were close. I think we should check it out. There's something more to this, I'm sure of it. Chottu wasn't just handing over a random address. He seemed to understand what we were talking about."

"Then why didn't he just tell us outright?" I asked, frustration creeping into my voice.

"Fear, maybe?" Manoj suggested. "You saw how nervous he was."

"So, do you want to go?" I asked tentatively. I hesitated to burden Manoj further, knowing this quest had been my pursuit.

"Get ready," he replied without missing a beat. "I'll pick you up in two hours."

His determination surprised me, infusing a shared sense of purpose into what had felt like a solitary mission. What had started as a personal endeavor now felt like a joint pursuit, Manoj's support a reassuring anchor in the uncertainty of our journey.

Two hours later, as I settled into Manoj's car, the weight of anticipation hung thick in the air.

"What do you think we'll find?" I asked, trying to mask my anxiety.

"No clue," Manoj replied. "Could be anything—or nothing. Let's not get our hopes too high."

I nodded, staring at the crumpled note in my hand. "What are we even going to say when we get there? We don't know who or what we're looking for."

Manoj chuckled. "We'll figure it out."

The car wound through Malviya Nagar and into narrower alleys as we approached Khirki. "This place is a maze," Manoj muttered, maneuvering past parked motorcycles and children playing cricket in the streets.

I showed the note to one of the boys. "Do you know where this address is?"

The boy glanced at it and shrugged. "I've lived here ten years. There's no house with this number."

"What the heck," I muttered, exasperated.

"Maybe it's a prank," Manoj said, his voice tinged with frustration.

"Could be, but the way Chottu gave me the note, it didn't seem random," I argued. Spotting a small alley, I asked the boy, "Is there a property dealer nearby?"

He pointed toward a shop further down. "Govind Properties. You could ask there."

Leaving Manoj with the car, I walked to the shop, nerves prickling at my skin.

After a few steps, I saw the faded signboard. It was a modest setup tucked into the corner of a bustling street, marked by a mesh of wires dangling precariously above. Inside, the cramped space was filled with mismatched furniture—a squeaky wooden desk, a couple of plastic chairs, and a rusty filing cabinet leaning against the wall. Piles of papers, dog-eared brochures, and yellowing property listings were scattered haphazardly, a testament to years of wheeling and dealing in the area.

The dealer himself was a wiry man in his late 40s, dressed in a worn-out shirt with the sleeves rolled up. His mobile phone, the lifeline of his trade, buzzed constantly as he juggled calls from potential clients and landlords.

"How can I help you?"

I handed him the note. "Do you know this address?"

He studied it, then shook his head. "Not in Khirki."

My heart sank.

"Wait…" His voice trailed off as he sifted through a bound file. Minutes later, he looked up with a triumphant smile. "Here it is. It's in Khirki Extension, not Khirki Village."

Relief and apprehension swirled within me. He rewrote the address with an addition and handed it over: B 16/22, Khirki Extension.

"Thank you," I said, pocketing the note.

"You are most welcome. Let me know if you want to buy or sell anything here. I am the most successful broker in this area."

I smiled, nodded, and waved him goodbye, certain that I may never see him again.

Back in the car, I narrated the exchange to Manoj.

"An extension? Seriously? This place has extensions?" Manoj quipped, shaking his head in disbelief.

We followed the new directions, parking the car, as the roads narrowed, a distance away from the colony gates Walking past faded signposts, we finally reached a building marked B-16/22, Khirki Extension.

I hesitated, my heart pounding. "What now?"

"Knock," Manoj urged.

I was hesitant not knowing what lay behind the closed doors. Would I be disappointed again or shocked? Would this be another dead end as it had turned out on all the previous instances?"

I summoned up the courage and knocked.

A female voice answered after what seemed like an eternity. I could hear steps coming closer, unlocking a latch as the door was flung open.

I wasn't sure how I had to react. Manoj clutched my shoulder, and I let out an inadvertent gasp.

In front of me stood Chottu from the paan shop in G.B. Road, his dark eyes alight with recognition.

"Who is it, Aman?" a woman's voice called from inside, tinged with apprehension.

Before we could respond, Nilofer appeared in the doorway. Her face froze as she saw us, her eyes darting between Chottu and me.

"Who are they?" came a gruff voice from within.

"Just some salesmen, Abba. They were leaving," Nilofer replied hastily, her voice tight with tension.

Chottu tugged at her sleeve, whispering something in her ear. Her expression shifted, torn between fear and defiance. There was an uncomfortable silence that was deafening.

Manoj nudged me. "We should go."

Before we could retreat, the man emerged—a figure that sent a jolt of recognition and dread through me. It was Sadiq Ali, the paanwallah from G.B. Road.

His eyes narrowed as he approached us almost as if trying to intimidate us. "Who are you, and what do you want?"

Caught off guard, Manoj and I exchanged a panicked glance. The stakes had just been raised, and the game had irrevocably changed.

Nilofer was staring at us and Chottu was subduing a smile, almost as if he had been victorious in achieving what he had intended to.

Chapter 23

Events were unfurling at an unexpected pace.

Aman, or "Chottu," hadn't just overheard our conversation at the paan shop—he had actively inserted himself into our story by providing a lead that we were still struggling to decipher. If his only intention had been to connect us with the paanwallah or himself, why take the risk of passing on the cryptic address?

Manoj and I had visited the paan shop before, but this time was different. Chottu's intense focus whenever Jannat was mentioned suggested he was more involved than we initially thought. By secretly slipping us the address, he had taken a bold and dangerous step, hinting at a deeper connection to Jannat's story.

Each new piece of the puzzle painted a more intricate picture—one in which Chottu seemed to play a pivotal role. His urgency, the clandestine way he passed us the address, and the fear in his eyes all pointed to a truth he wanted us to uncover. The quest for Jannat had taken yet another turn, and we were on the brink of uncovering the next layer.

Could I find Jannat here? I wondered. No, that can't be possible.

"What do you want?" The paanwallah's gruff voice pulled me back to reality. Nilofer quickly joined him, her face unreadable.

"We need to talk," I replied firmly. "It's important."

The paanwallah's demeanor was cold, a stark contrast to the nicety he displayed at his shop. "Why have you followed me here?" he asked, his suspicion directed more at Nilofer than at us.

I decided to take the offensive. "You remember we came looking for a girl named Jannat," I said, keeping my voice steady. "You claimed not to know her, but we believe you do."

The silence that followed was suffocating. Nilofer let out a sharp gasp before hurrying out of the room. The paanwallah stood frozen, his face a mask of shock and denial.

Manoj glanced at me, his expression a mix of disbelief and confusion. The weight of my accusation hung in the air, the tension palpable as if we had unleashed a secret too heavy for the room to bear.

"Who are you, and how did you get my address?" the paanwallah finally demanded, his voice quivering with barely concealed anger.

"We're her brothers," I lied. "We came to Delhi years ago looking for her and even filed an FIR at the police station."

"Who gave you this address?" His agitation grew, the friendly facade from the shop completely gone.

"We found it," Manoj interjected, his tone turning aggressive. "And we know she came here."

The paanwallah's shoulders sagged slightly as though resigning himself to the inevitable. He motioned for us to enter, perhaps hoping to shield the conversation from prying ears.

Inside, the atmosphere was stifling. He sat down, his voice heavy with bitterness. "What can I tell you? She doesn't live here anymore. She ran away within a week of coming here, with some boy from the neighborhood. That girl had no gratitude. I saved her from that hellhole, and this is how she repaid me."

Chottu appeared as he made his way past us through the door with a bag in his hand. He did not acknowledge us."

Sadiq Ali's words dripped with resentment, his version of events portraying Jannat as ungrateful and rebellious. "I bought her from Neerja bi, who needed money. I didn't want her to live that life anymore. I thought I could provide her with a home, maybe even some education. She could've been company for my daughter, Nilofer. But no—she ran away."

"Ran away with a boy?" I repeated, skeptical. "That doesn't sound like Jannat."

"Believe what you want," he said dismissively. "I didn't file a missing person report either—why invite unnecessary attention? What's done is done."

"Which boy did she run away with?" I pressed.

"Some garbage picker or helper from the street. Who knows? She wanted a different life and didn't trust me to give it to her. Maybe she's dead by now."

Manoj leaned forward. "If you're lying, we'll be back—with the authorities this time."

The paanwallah's eyes darkened, but he said nothing. His silence was enough to convince us that this thread had unraveled.

We walked out of the house, the door slamming shut behind us. Manoj put a comforting arm around my shoulders. "It's okay, man. At least you tried. God bless her, wherever she is."

"Do you believe what he said?" I asked

"How does it matter? There is no other way to find out and Chottu just walked away. This must be some kind of a joke. Leading us all the way here only to let us know that Jannat has run away with somebody."

I sighed in exasperation. As we reached the colony gate, Chottu appeared from the opposite direction with the vegetable part sticking out from the bag that he had left the house with. His expression shifted to one of disappointment as he realized, from our demeanor, that our visit had yielded no answers. Yet, there was something in his eyes—a quiet determination.

He held my hand, his grip firm. "Nofofa nos," he muttered, his voice low.

The cryptic word caught me off guard. "What does that mean?" I asked, leaning closer.

Chottu glanced over his shoulder, his fear palpable. Before he could explain, he froze. His eyes widened in terror as he looked past my shoulder. The vegetables slipped from his hand as he scrambled to put the potatoes back into the bag and bolted back toward the house.

The paanwallah was standing at the gate, watching us leave. His expression was unreadable, but the tension between him and Chottu was undeniable as Chottu scrambled past him into the confines of the house.

We went past the gate and turned towards our car which was parked on the turn. As we approached the car, I felt a presence behind me. Turning, I was stunned to see the figure before me, a familiar one.

It was Nilofer.

"Meet me at the Sai Computer Centre behind Om Sweets tomorrow at 11 a.m.," she said hurriedly, her voice barely above a whisper even before I could open my mouth.

"Wait!" I called after her. "Why do you want to meet us? What do you know?"

She stopped briefly. "I know where Jannat is, and I can help you find her."

Before I could respond, she disappeared into the maze of narrow lanes, leaving Manoj and me standing under the streetlamps, stunned.

"What just happened?" I wondered.

"Let's leave now buddy," Manoj said. Sadiq may suspect something so let's go before he decides to walk our way."

I had to agree and quickly got into the car.

As we drove away, the weight of her revelation settled on us. Nilofer held the key to Jannat's whereabouts. The cryptic trail that had led us here suddenly seemed purposeful.

"Tomorrow," I muttered to myself. "We'll get our answers tomorrow."

Chottu was right. Nilofer knows.

Chapter 24

Manoj, clearly worn out from all the running around I had subjected him to, called me later that evening. "Do you mind meeting Nilofer alone tomorrow? I feel like I've been neglecting everything else in my life for this chase."

I understood where he was coming from. After all, he had a life to return to, unlike me, who seemed to have temporarily lost sight of my own.

"Of course, Manoj. Don't worry about it. I'll meet her and fill you in afterward," I replied.

"Thanks, buddy. Let me know what happens." His voice carried both relief and lingering curiosity before he hung up.

The next morning, I arrived at Malviya Nagar around 10:30, unsure of what awaited me. The doubts gnawed at me as I made my way to Sai Computer Centre. What if the paanwallah sent Nilofer to lure me to a prearranged spot to silence me? I wondered. The thought was unsettling, and I wished Manoj were there.

But then I reassured myself: It's broad daylight, with plenty of people around. That kind of thing doesn't happen in the middle of a bustling market, right?

The market was waking up in its usual chaotic fashion. Bikers wove dangerously through narrow lanes meant for pedestrians, and shoppers strolled along streets meant for vehicles. After asking for directions a few times, I found myself standing in front of a decrepit shop. A peeling sign announced: SAI COMPUTER CENTRE.

I checked my watch. 11:10. "Where is she?" I muttered, scanning the bustling scene around me. "Had she been caught out by her father and confined at home?"

"Adaab, Bhaijaan."

The voice from behind startled me, though I instinctively knew who it was. Turning, I saw Nilofer, her expression wary, her eyes scanning the surroundings.

"Adaab," I replied.

She motioned toward a tree beside a shop and whispered, "Let's stand over there. It's less exposed."

The marketplace was coming alive. Vegetable vendors were setting up their carts, tempos fought for every inch of space, and a cacophony of bargaining echoed around us. As we moved beside the shop, I noticed Nilofer more closely. Despite her youth—she couldn't have been older than her late teens—her face bore the unmistakable signs of a difficult life. It was evident that she had weathered many a personal storm in her life and was consciously wading into another one.

"You're looking for Jannat?" she began without wasting a moment, her voice low but direct. "I don't have much time, so I'll speak quickly."

"Yes," I said, my voice betraying my eagerness. Finally, someone who might have real answers.

She nodded and pulled out a book from her bag almost like a decoy. She opened the book and started showing me some pages. The deception was complete. "Jannat was with us about a year ago. My father brought her home. I took to her instantly and saw her as a younger sister. She shared her pain with me, and we grew close. Her stories... they broke me." Nilofer's voice faltered, and tears welled up in her eyes. She tried to hold them back, but her struggle was obvious.

I felt awkward as the silence stretched. Part of me wanted to comfort her, but I wasn't sure if it would be appropriate.

"So, why did she run away if you cared so much for her?" I asked gently.

"She didn't run away," Nilofer said, her voice suddenly firm. "My father lied to you."

"Oh my God?" I muttered under my breath, caught off guard.

Nilofer continued, her words heavy with suppressed anger. "My father isn't the man he pretends to be. He buys girls like Jannat and sells them to older men—sometimes here, sometimes abroad. He's part of a racket. They come to our house or meet him elsewhere, and the girls disappear. No one knows what happens to them. He hides all this behind the guise of a paan shop on G.B. Road. Who would suspect a thing? A simple paan shop."

Her revelations hit like a punch to the gut. The bustling market around us became a backdrop of chaos that seemed almost fitting for the grim truths she was exposing.

She hesitated, her face flushed with shame and anger. "Jannat stayed with us for about ten months. Over time, she started looking healthier, happier even. We bonded deeply. But then..."

She stopped, looking around nervously. Her composure faltered as the weight of her story bore down on her.

"But then what?" I prompted, my impatience slipping through.

"One day, a friend of my father's came for dinner. He saw Jannat and took a liking to her. He asked my father to let her go with him. At first, my father refused, but the man offered a lot of money. Eventually, he gave in." She wiped a tear from her cheek and continued, her voice trembling. "The next day, the man came and took her. Jannat cried and pleaded not to go, but it didn't matter. The deal was done."

I felt a pit forming in my stomach. "And then?"

"We visited his house in Sant Nagar a couple of times after that," she said, her voice breaking. "We never saw her again. He runs a restaurant there. I don't want to know what happened to her. I can't bear to think about it." She paused, visibly shaken, then added, "You wouldn't have heard about Jannat if you hadn't come looking. She's just… gone."

I tried to process her words. "Do you know where this man lives or where his restaurant is? I must try and find her."

Nilofer hesitated, then nodded. "His restaurant is called Saleem's. It's at A-24, Sant Nagar, next to the East of Kailash. But I don't think you'll find her there. We asked about her once, but he dodged the questions."

"What about Chottu?" I asked. "Aman has been instrumental in helping us get this far. What's his connection to all this?"

Nilofer's expression softened. "He's her brother," she said quietly.

Her words landed like a revelation, adding another layer to the intricate web surrounding Jannat.

"You're a good man," she said after a pause. "I can tell you care about Jannat, but… please don't chase her anymore. What do you hope to achieve? To bring her into your world? She doesn't want that. She's built two worlds for herself—one to survive, one to find peace. Don't destroy them because you think they need saving. To her, your world doesn't exist. If anything, you might put her in more danger."

Her words were both a warning and a plea. They stung, but they also carried a strange wisdom.

"Khuda Hafiz," Nilofer said quietly, stepping away from the tree. "I need to go before my computer teacher calls home to report my absence. I'll have to make up an excuse to avoid suspicion."

"I can't thank you enough for what you've shared," I said. "Take care of Aman. And even if you don't want me to look for Jannat, don't you want to know if she's alive and well?"

Nilofer didn't answer.

"I really must go now," she said, walking briskly toward the Sai Computer Centre. She glanced back once, her expression unreadable, before vanishing around the corner.

I stood there, rooted in place, trying to process the cascade of revelations. The paanwallah's betrayal, Nilofer's courage, and the cryptic clue left by Neerja Bi all clicked together like pieces of a sinister puzzle. "Sabhi ek doosre ko choona laga rahein hai yahaan." Neerja's words echoed in my mind, their meaning now painfully clear. The paanwallah, with his seemingly innocuous trade, was a predator, and I had missed the signs.

Nilofer's parting words echoed in my mind: Aman is her brother, and Jannat has made peace with her world.

Chapter 25

Aman had stumbled into this life by accident, lured by his uncle from Sonagachi with the promise of reuniting with his sister, Jannat. She had been taken away when Aman was barely five years old, and she was seven. The memories of that fateful night lingered in his mind like shadows, stretching across the years, relentless in their grip on his heart.

That night had been a whirlwind of tears and heartache as he overheard his parents speak in hushed tones. He had pretended to be asleep, but the subdued conversation almost shattered his eardrums. It was the night his family made a choice dictated by poverty, leaving Aman to grapple with a reality he could neither control nor fully understand.

"How did we let it come to this? I work from dawn till dusk, but it's never enough. We're drowning, and no one even notices." It was his father.

"It's not your fault. It's just... this world isn't kind to people like us. But Amu... he deserves better. We can't let him grow up like this, without a future. Jannat is doing well I am sure and perhaps we need to let him go as well rather than live in the living hell."

Aman could sense that his father was choking up. "Do you think I don't know that? He's a bright kid. He dreams so big. But dreams don't put food on the table. They don't pay school fees. What choice do we have?"

"We have to let him go. Maybe they can give him a chance we can't. Maybe he'll understand someday… but it's going to break his heart." His mother said as she sobbed.

"It's breaking mine too. He's, my son. How can I send him away? But keeping him here… we'll ruin him. He'll hate us for this, won't he?"

"He might. For a while but one day, he'll see why we did it. At least, I pray he will."

Aman remained silent with his eyes closed. silence. "What are they saying? They're sending me away. Why? What did I do wrong? I don't understand…"

After a long pause, his father continued "We'll explain it to him tomorrow. Somehow. Tonight… let's just get through this."

He heard his mother's last words through her tears. "I hope he forgives us."

As Aman listened silently, his chest tightened with a mix of confusion and pain. It was a night of whispers and sobs that marked the unraveling of his childhood innocence, leaving behind questions too heavy for his young heart to carry.

The separation had left a void, an aching absence in their home. His family's struggle to make ends meet had devoid them of any emotion. Leaving them with no choice but to view their children as burdens or, in the case of his sisters, potential commodities. Born with a speech deformity that made communication difficult, Aman had been deemed unfit for the world's brutal demands.

He had cried himself to sleep countless nights, haunted by thoughts of his worthlessness. If only he could speak like other children, perhaps his family might have looked upon him with kinder eyes. Aman's disability rendered him invisible in a family that could barely hold itself together. His only value, it seemed, was in being forgotten.

Sometime later when his uncle suggested a trip to Delhi to see Jannat, Aman had leaped at the opportunity, his heart brimming with hope. His parents, relieved at the chance to rid themselves of him, barely hesitated. Unbeknownst to Aman, his uncle had other motives, seeing him as a potential saleable asset and having sealed a fair deal with his parents which would see them through for another 5-6 months.

When they arrived in Delhi, the paanwallah was their first stop.

The paanwallah, who had already purchased Jannat, saw an opportunity to take Aman as well. A boy to help with the shop and keep Jannat company—it was a deal too good to pass up. When Aman first saw his sister, he cried out, "Didee!" and rushed to embrace her. The siblings' reunion was fierce and raw, their bond immediately apparent to everyone.

Nilofer had been overjoyed by Aman's arrival. For her, Jannat and Aman's presence filled the emptiness in her life, giving her a semblance of the family she longed for. But her happiness was short-lived.

Eight months later, Jannat was taken away. Nilofer had pleaded with her father, and Aman had tried to convey his heartbreak in the only ways he could, but their protests fell on deaf ears.

"I'm not here to create a family," the paanwallah had said coldly. "She'll be taken care of. The boy can stay and work."

"What about what I want?" Nilofer had demanded, her voice trembling with rage and despair.

"Your wishes mean nothing to me," Sadiq Ali had replied.

Nilofer despised him more with each passing day, and a part of her feared that Aman, the one person who seemed to feel the loss as deeply as she did, might one day take matters into his own hands. There is nothing more dangerous than a person who has nothing to lose, and Aman has nothing left to lose.

Chapter 26

Sant Nagar was next. I needed to know if Manoj was willing to come along. Checking my phone, I saw three missed calls from him.

"Manoj bhai," I said, returning his call.

"Where have you been, man? I've been trying to reach you. What's going on?"

I quickly recounted everything Nilofer had told me, and Manoj listened silently.

"When can we meet?" I asked hesitantly.

"An hour. I'm finishing up some stuff in Greater Kailash. Let's grab lunch. Saleem's Restaurant in Sant Nagar. What do you say?" he said and let out a laugh.

The name caught me off guard. "That's... perfect. Let's do it."

For the first time all day, I smiled. The pieces of the puzzle were falling into place, and I felt the closure I'd been chasing for so long might finally be within reach.

As we drove toward Sant Nagar, I couldn't shake the feeling that this journey, with all its strange patterns and twists, was far from over.

Jannat remained elusive as ever. Yet as the story was unfolding it was pulling us deeper into its tangled web.

An hour and a half later, Manoj's car pulled up behind mine. I stepped out, waved, and got into his car. He always preferred to drive.

"What's up, dude? Seems like you've had quite the morning. There are so many players in this now. If that paanwallah finds out Nilofer and Chottu have been giving you clues, I'm not sure what he'd do to them." Manoj's voice carried both concern and weariness as I buckled my seatbelt.

"That's true," I replied. "It's all so chaotic. Just cannot understand." I paused, gazing out the window as we started toward Sant Nagar.

"It's not far from Malviya Nagar," Manoj observed, and soon enough, he pointed to a large green sign atop a bamboo structure. "There it is."

The sign read make curly Saleem Dhaba', mounted prominently by the main road. My heart raced as Manoj parked the car beneath it.

I stepped out, lit a Marlboro Light, and glanced around. "Looks decent, doesn't it?" I asked Manoj, exhaling smoke.

"Yeah, seems like it's doing well," he replied.

Saleem's Dhaba exuded a clean and spacious ambiance, a welcoming sight for anyone seeking a quick, satisfying meal. Despite its simplicity, the place carried an unpretentious charm, with its neat arrangement of tables and the earthy warmth of its décor. Located on the ground floor of a modest building, it was easily accessible, a feature that contributed to its steady stream of regular patrons.

Sturdy metal tables stood neatly aligned in rows, their tops covered with colorful, wipeable plastic sheets featuring floral or checkered patterns. Each table was flanked by matching chairs. A few tables were slightly larger, accommodating groups, while smaller ones provided a cozy setting for individuals or pairs.

The air was infused with the heady fragrance of spices, an irresistible blend of cardamom, and cumin, and the smoky aroma of tandoori dishes being prepared in the open kitchen. The smell of fresh coriander mingled with the rich, buttery essence of dal makhani and the tangy undertones of sizzling onions and tomatoes being cooked to perfection.

Its ground-floor location offered easy access, ensuring a steady clientele. At nearly 3 p.m., the lull of the afternoon was evident. The usual buzz of voices and clinking utensils had faded, leaving the space mostly quiet. Only a small group of five boys occupied a table in the far corner, their animated chatter occasionally breaking the stillness. Their laughter and the occasional clatter of plates were the only signs of life in an otherwise quiet setting.

A boy approached us, a rag slung over his shoulder.

"The dhaba is closed sahib," he said while clearing a nearby table.

Not to be outdone, I countered "Can we at least get our roti and daal? We are hungry, and we'll tip you well," I offered, handing him a fifty-rupee note.

The boy smiled and placed a laminated menu in front of us. "Order quickly. Sahib will be here any minute, and he doesn't like it when I appear too helpful. He doesn't trust anyone," he muttered bitterly.

"How long have you been working here?" I asked, though Manoj seemed visibly irritated—he was starving.

"Too long, sahib, but I'm still treated like a servant."

"What's your name?"

"Deepak, but everyone calls me Chottu."

Manoj intervened, his hunger overtaking his patience. "Listen, get us some roti and black dal fry. Four rotis for now. That can be done, right?"

Chottu nodded and disappeared into the kitchen.

After what felt like an eternity, Chottu returned with two plates and a steaming bowl of dal, followed by four piping-hot tandoori rotis. He placed everything on the table and turned to leave, but I stopped him.

"There's something we need to ask you."

"What is it, sahib? There's nothing left in the kitchen, and you can't drink here."

Before I could continue, the boys at the other end called out to him and signaled for their bill. Chottu scribbled a slip, handed it to them, and returned to our table after collecting the payment.

"Yes, sahib? Now tell me. What were you asking?"

"Does a girl named Jannat work here?" I asked bluntly.

Manoj froze mid-bite, his hunger momentarily forgotten.

Chottu hesitated, fear flashing across his face. He stared at me, his mouth agape almost as if I had uttered a bad curse. I pulled out a hundred-rupee note. "Tell me, and there's more where this came from."

The boy glanced nervously around before reaching out to pocket the hundred-rupee note. "Yes, sahib. I know her, but how do you know her?

"That's not important," Manoj responded. "You just tell us what we need to know, and you will walk away with lots of money."

That seemed to work.

"She is not here anymore, sahib."

"What?" My voice rose in disbelief, but Manoj placed a calming hand on my shoulder.

"She was here," Chottu continued. "Saleem sahib brought her here. She helped in the kitchen during the day and cleaned tables. At night…" He trailed off, glancing toward the kitchen, his face clouded with discomfort.

"What happened next?" I urged.

"One night, a group of boys came in for dinner. One of them, Rahul bhaiyya, started talking to her. They came often after that, always asking for her. She'd speak to him only when Saleem sahib wasn't around. He had forbidden her from talking to anyone."

"Was there something between them?" Manoj asked.

Chottu shook his head. "No, sahib. Rahul bhaiyya was different. He asked about her family and if she was being forced to work. He promised to help her. One night, when Saleem sahib was away, Rahul bhaiyya came with an uncle and aunty. I helped her into their car, and they drove off. I haven't seen her since."

"How do you know she's okay?"

"Rahul bhaiyya still comes here sometimes. He shows me pictures of her. She looks happy."

My heart lifted slightly. "Can you let me know the next time they visit?"

"Yes, sahib, but how will I contact you?"

I turned to Manoj. "Do you still have that flip phone in your car?"

Manoj got up and walked towards the exit door and returned a few moments later with the phone and handed it to me. I gave it to Chottu along with a charger. "Call me when they're here next."

Chottu nodded, delighted at the prospect of owning a mobile phone.

"If only you had come in an hour ago." He said making sure the phone and its charger were safely tucked away in the pocket of his grimy trousers. "You had have asked them yourself. They were just here,"

"What?"

"Yes, sahib. The boy in the blue shirt who paid the bill just some moments ago was Rahul bhaiyya."

Before I could process this revelation, I heard a car screech to a halt outside the dhaba.

"That's Saleem," Chottu whispered, his voice trembling. "Please, sahib, don't say anything."

"We won't," I assured him, slipping him another hundred. "Thank you for everything."

As we got up to leave, we heard the door open and in walked Saleem. He was an intimidating figure, and he moved with a confidence that bordered on arrogance. His rugged face bore the marks of a hard life—deep-set eyes that seemed to pierce rather than look, a furrowed brow, and a jagged scar running from his temple to his cheek. His thick, unkempt beard added to his intimidating aura, and his booming voice could silence a room with a single barked order. He was a man who exuded authority and menace.

We passed by him and headed to our car.

As we got in, Manoj sighed. "How much longer before we can let this go?"

I didn't answer. The truth felt close, yet Jannat remained as elusive as ever.

Chapter 27

In the stifling confines of the paan shop and the house in Khirki Extn. Three lives intertwined in a delicate trinity: the paanwallah, Nilofer, and Chottu. Each bore their burden, their roles distinct yet inextricably linked by the threads of circumstance and fate.

The paanwallah was an imposing figure, his gruff demeanor amplified by the stale scent of betel leaves and tobacco that clung to the air. Every puff of his beedi seemed to assert his dominance.

Chottu, though small in stature and burdened with a speech deformity, carried an unexpected strength beneath his exterior. His eyes, ever watchful, reflected a blend of fear and resilience. He had learned to navigate the stormy temperament of the paanwallah, enduring the harsh words and occasional blows with a quiet resolve bordering on helplessness.

And then there was Nilofer, standing at the intersection of these two worlds. She bore witness to her father's cruelty and Chottu's silent suffering, her pain simmering beneath a stoic facade.

The afternoon was oppressive, the heat outside was seeping into the walls of the house. The water cooler was running at full speed but did little to remove the humidity in the air. Nilofer was crouched near the counter, playing with Chottu, whose laughter momentarily brightened the otherwise dismal space. Their brief respite was shattered by the arrival of the paanwallah, his sour mood trailing behind.

He dropped himself heavily onto the sofa, his face a mask of irritation. "Get my bottle from the cupboard inside," he barked at Chottu. "And don't forget the soda and ice!"

Chottu scrambled to obey, his small frame moving with the urgency of someone well-acquainted with the consequences of delay. Fear etched his every move as he reappeared, carefully balancing a tray laden with a bottle, soda, and glass. He placed it before the paanwallah, standing still, waiting for the next order.

Nilofer watched silently from the corner, her gaze unwavering as it bore into her father. Her disdain was evident, a quiet rebellion simmering beneath the surface.

"Go boil some eggs and get chana, you lazy lout!" the paanwallah barked, waving his hand in a motion that promised a slap. Chottu fled to the kitchen, leaving behind the tension that hung in the air.

"You have to stop treating him like this, Abba," Nilofer said, her voice calm but firm.

"I don't need lessons from you," he snapped. "Now get out and let me drink in peace."

Nilofer left the room, retreating to the kitchen where she found Chottu peeling boiled eggs, his shoulders shaking with silent sobs. The sight pierced her, a reflection of her helplessness. She placed a hand on his back, her touch a small but meaningful gesture of comfort.

"Come, let me help you," she said, picking up an egg.

Chottu turned toward her and hugged her tightly, his tears soaking into her shoulder. "I sury, Didee," he mumbled, his words tinged with both guilt and pain.

"For what, Amu? You've done nothing wrong," she reassured him. "It's just the situation we're in. We can't change it, no matter how hard we try."

Chottu pulled back, his tear-streaked face shining with an emotion Nilofer couldn't quite place. There was a spark in his eyes—a determined, almost defiant glimmer that hadn't been there before.

Unbeknownst to Nilofer, Chottu's apology had been more than an expression of remorse. It had been a precursor to a decision—a silent promise to himself that he would not remain a pawn to be abused every day.

As he returned to peeling the eggs, a quiet determination settled over him. Nilofer could sense something stirring within the boy, though she couldn't yet understand the depths of his resolve. Suspense hung thick in the air, an unspoken promise of change that Nilofer could not foresee.

In this small, suffocating world, a storm was brewing. A silent but powerful rebellion that would alter the dynamics of their fragile trinity forever.

Chapter 28

The weeks of waiting had stretched my patience thin. It had been three weeks since I'd last met Chottu at Saleem's restaurant and handed him the phone. Despite his assurances, no call had come.

"What do you think happened?" I asked Manoj, Abhay, and Sunil, who were gathered at my place for a stag night. With Shayna away visiting friends in the U.S., the evening had taken on a more casual and indulgent tone, with drinks flowing freely and conversations veering in every direction.

"These people are all the same," Abhay said dismissively, swirling his drink. "He's probably sold off the phone and spent the money. I've seen it before. One time, I gave a family some rations—flour, rice, oil, the basics. What did they do? Sold it to the corner shop for cash."

"Not everyone's like that," Sunil countered.

"Almost everyone is," Abhay insisted, taking another sip.

I couldn't help but check my phone every few minutes, hoping for a call or even a message. The silence was maddening.

"I kind of agree with Abhay," Manoj added "Cash is just more tempting. They don't think long-term."

As the conversation shifted to other topics, including Abhay's absurd plan for some "action" in a hotel room, I couldn't shake my growing unease. I glanced at Manoj and smiled faintly, trying to stay present, but my mind kept drifting back to Chottu, Nilofer, and the tangled mess we'd gotten ourselves into.

Meanwhile, at the flat in Khirki Extension, the air was thick with tension.

"Get me some soda, you useless brat!" the paanwallah barked.

Chottu flinched but obeyed, his fear palpable. Nilofer, ever the silent observer, handed him a plate with half-cut boiled eggs and a soda bottle.

"Here, take this to him," she said gently.

Chottu placed the items before the paanwallah, only to be met with another volley of insults. "What took you so long? Where are the onions?"

Chottu noticed that the bottle was almost empty. The paanwallah had pulled out all the stops tonight.

"I will get them now," said Chottu.

Nilofer heard what her father had to say and quickly took out two large raw onions from the vegetable basket and looked around for the knife and the chaat masala.

"Now listen, you piece of shit. Do not think you are part of the family even though Nilofer treats you like one." Nilofer could hear her father admonish Chottu yet again.

"Aman, come here," Nilofer called her voice in a desperate attempt to shield Chottu from further abuse. She wanted to cut the onions and tomatoes, sprinkle some masala, and hand it over to him before her father let loose another volley of abuses at Chottu. She searched for the knife but it was nowhere to be found.

There was no response and everything seemed quiet. She called out to Aman again and apart from some guttural sounds there was no other response from the living room. She then heard the glass and possibly the bottle fall to the floor and break. Fearing the worst for Aman, Nilofer rushed out of the kitchen and entered the living room.

She gasped in horror at the sight before her.

Aman stood behind the paanwallah, his hand gripping the man's head back, while a knife was clenched in the other. Nilofer cautiously moved closer, her eyes widening as she faced the unfolding scene. The paanwallah lay on the sofa, writhing in agony, desperately trying to free himself. Blood gushed from a deep cut inflicted on the neck by the knife in Aman's hand, staining the man's shirt and the sofa beneath.

The room reeked of betel leaves and blood, the fluorescent light flickering as if in protest. The paanwallah's attempts to stem the bleeding were futile; his severed vocal cords rendered his pleas soundless. The T.V. playing some Hindi song remixes in high volume.

Nilofer, rooted to the spot, felt the weight of the moment crush her. Every insult, every act of violence her father had inflicted, seemed to culminate in this grotesque tableau.

She moved closer, her body trembling but her resolve hardening. With a grim determination, she held down her father's arms, ensuring he could no longer fight. Aman maintained his grip, his face a mask of vengeance and pain.

The struggle lasted only moments, though it felt like an eternity. Aman then let go and looked at Nilofer as he dropped the knife.

She reached out to him and held him by his shoulders as she pulled him towards her in a tight embrace.

Aman and Nilofer collapsed into each other's arms, their sobs breaking the oppressive silence.

The flat, once a stage for the paanwallah's reign of terror, was now a scene of irrevocable change. The trinity that had defined this space—the oppressor, the survivor, and the silent witness—had been shattered, leaving behind only two: Nilofer and Aman, bound together by shared pain and an act of irreversible defiance.

As they clung to each other, their tears carried the weight of years of abuse, fear, and unspoken anger. And yet, amidst the horror, there was a glimmer of something else: freedom.

For the first time in years, the oppressive shadow of the paanwallah no longer loomed over them.

But at what cost?

Chapter 29

The shrill ring of my phone pierced the stillness of the night, dragging me from my thoughts. At first, I ignored it, dismissing it as yet another spam call. But the persistence of the ringing nudged me into action.

"Yes, who is this?" I barked into the phone, my irritation unmistakable.

"Saab, it's me, Chottu," came the hurried voice on the other end.

Chottu. The name jolted me awake. "Chottu? Where have you been? I've been wai—"

"The boys are here, saab," Chottu cut me off mid-sentence. "How quickly can you get here?"

My pulse quickened. "I can be there in 45 minutes. Traffic will be light this late."

"Come quickly, saab. They just walked in, so they'll be here for another hour at least. I called you as soon as they came."

"Good. I'm on my way."

Hanging up, I turned to Manoj. "We need to leave now," I said, grabbing my jacket.

Abhay, seated comfortably with a drink in hand, raised an eyebrow. "What's the rush? You can't just ditch us!"

"It's Jannat. The boys who were last seen with her are at Saleem's dhaba. This might be our only shot," I explained hurriedly.

Sunil, less accusatory, asked, "Should we wait for you to come back?"

"No idea how long this will take. Stay and enjoy yourselves. There's food in the kitchen, and the servant will help you with anything you need."

I grabbed the car keys and motioned for Manoj to follow.

Once inside the car, Manoj groaned. "I've had too much to drink, man."

"That's fine. I'll drive," I replied, starting the engine.

We sped through the quiet streets, the urgency palpable. Manoj, still processing the situation, asked, "So what's the plan? Walk up to the guy and demand answers?"

I didn't respond, my focus was fixed on the road. Time was slipping away, and every second felt critical.

As we approached Malviya Nagar, our progress came to an abrupt halt. A line of cars stretched ahead, a police checkpoint illuminated by harsh lights.

"Damn it," Manoj muttered.

As our car neared the checkpoint, a police constable motioned us to pull aside and gestured with his hands to roll the window down.

As I politely complied, an officer made his way to our car armed with a breathalyzer.

"Have you guys been drinking?" he asked, his gaze sharp.

"A little," I admitted, knowing honesty was my best bet.

"License and car papers," he demanded.

Manoj intervened with a fabricated story. "Sir, we're heading to the station to pick up his elderly father. He's nearly 90 and can't be left waiting in the cold."

The officer wasn't buying it. "And you thought drinking was a good idea before driving to meet him?"

Sensing the situation escalating, Manoj pulled out his Delhi charm offensive, "Sir, can we work something out?"

The officer's eyes sparkled. "Five thousand," the officer said without hesitation.

"Two thousand," Manoj countered.

"You think I am a bloody beggar." He said clearly beginning to lose his patience. Manoj apologized and expressed helplessness as that was all we had. After a tense pause, the officer relented. "Fine. Now get out of here."

I handed over the money and drove off, the delay gnawing at me.

We arrived at Saleem's dhaba just before 11 p.m. My heart sank as I scanned the area—no BMW, no boys.

Inside, Chottu was busy serving customers but noticed us immediately. His expression gave nothing away as he gestured for us to sit.

"What will you have, saab?" Chottu asked, his tone polite but distant.

"Roti, daal, and a mutton dish," Manoj ordered, attempting to mask his frustration. Something had to be ordered to serve the purpose of a smoke screen.

Chottu nodded, subtly winking at me before heading to the kitchen.

As we waited, a commotion broke out near the billing counter. Saleem, visibly agitated, was on the phone. His voice cut through the air, sharp and urgent.

"This can't be true. Who did this? I'm coming right away," he declared, slamming the phone down and rushing out.

Chottu hurried to our table once Saleem had left.

"Thank God he's gone," Chottu said, his voice low. "You took too long. I told you to come urgently. The boys have already left."

I felt the weight of his words settle heavily in my chest. "We were delayed because of the cops," I reasoned "Is there any other lead?" I began to ask, but Chottu had already turned away, attending to another table.

Manoj, sensing my frustration, leaned back in his chair. "Maybe it's time to let this go. We've been chasing shadows for weeks. It's draining, and frankly, we're not making any progress."

I couldn't argue with him. Every lead seemed to end in disappointment.

We decided not to wait for the food and rejoin our friends whom we had left behind in our mad dash to meet with the boys. Just as we were preparing to leave, Chottu returned, an unexpected smile on his face.

"Guess what? You're lucky tonight. One of the boys will be back shortly—they forgot their phone here."

The sudden hope was electrifying. "That's great news!"

There was, however, something else on Chottu's mind as he leaned closer, his tone conspiratorial. "Tell me truthfully. Did you guys have anything to do with the murder of the man who sold Jannat to Saleem?"

The question hung in the air, heavy with implication. For a moment, I was at a loss for words, unsure how to navigate the unexpected turn this night had taken.

`Who, Sadiq?" I asked.

Chottu nodded, not entirely sure if he could trust us any longer.

Chapter 30

The revelation struck us like a thunderclap, shattering the fragile calm that had momentarily settled over Saleem's dhaba. The weight of Chottu's words bore down on us, heavy and unrelenting, leaving Manoj and me grappling with a flood of unanswered questions.

"Murder?" I repeated, the disbelief thick in my voice. My heart pounded as I tried to process the enormity of what I'd just heard. "Are you saying the Sadiq was murdered?"

"Yes, saab," Chottu replied, his tone laced with an unsettling mix of intrigue and nonchalance. "Saleem mentioned it before he left. The paanwallah—his friend, the one who sold Jannat to him—was murdered. Someone slashed his throat. He bled to death."

The words hung in the air, their grim finality sending a chill down my spine. I exchanged a glance with Manoj, his furrowed brow reflecting the same unease that churned within me. The paanwallah's death was not just a random act of violence; it carried with it an undercurrent of sinister intent, weaving itself into the tangled web of Jannat's story.

"What about Nilofer and Aman?" I blurted out, the urgency in my voice betraying the panic I felt at the thought of their safety. "Do you think they're in danger?"

Chottu tilted his head, a cryptic smile playing on his lips. "Saab, I don't know who Nilofer and Aman are. I told you about this because you're so interested in Jannat. For a moment, I wondered if you had something to do with it. But looking at your reaction… I guess not."

The juxtaposition of his calm demeanor with the macabre news sent a wave of unease rippling through me. The usual background hum of the dhaba—the clinking of plates, distant laughter, and the sizzle of food being cooked—seemed jarringly out of place against the weight of the revelation.

Manoj broke the silence, his voice steady but tinged with apprehension. "So, someone killed the paanwallah. But why? And how does this tie into Jannat?"

Chottu leaned in slightly, his eyes darting around as if to ensure no one else was listening. "That's what Saleem said. The paanwallah was the one who sold Jannat to him. Saleem was rushing to see the family. They have known each other for years."

The statement landed heavily, connecting yet another thread to the labyrinthine narrative surrounding Jannat's disappearance. A sense of foreboding settled over us as we tried to come to terms with the implications of the murder.

"This is getting darker by the minute," Manoj muttered, his unease palpable. "First Jannat, now this. Are we sure they aren't connected?"

Chottu shrugged, his voice low. "Saab, in this world, anything is possible. Sometimes, the connections are there, even if we can't see them."

We sat in silence, each lost in our thoughts. The prospect of the boys returning to retrieve their forgotten mobile suddenly took on a new weight. This wasn't just about a misplaced device—it was an opportunity to delve deeper into the murky waters that seemed to swirl around Saleem, the paanwallah, and Jannat.

The aroma of food wafted up from the table, untouched and forgotten during our escalating tension. Every passing minute felt like an eternity.

"They should be here any minute now," Chottu said, glancing toward the entrance. "Just act normal, saab."

The warning underscored the fragile nature of our position. The night had taken a chilling turn, steering us into uncharted territory. With every step deeper into this narrative, the stakes grew higher, and the threads of the story became increasingly tangled.

The quest for Jannat had led us into the heart of darkness, and as the shadows deepened around Saleem's dhaba, the truth felt closer than ever—poised to reveal itself in ways we might not have been prepared for.

Chapter 31

The car screeched to a halt outside Saleem's for the second time that night, its arrival shattering the stillness of the late hour. A boy emerged from the sleek vehicle, his face a cocktail of irritation and urgency. Without glancing back, he strode briskly into the restaurant, leaving the others cocooned in the chilled luxury of the BMW.

The creak of the restaurant door echoed in the near-empty space as the boy entered, his presence altering the atmosphere. Tension simmered in the air as he approached Chottu, who promptly handed him the forgotten phone. The boy retrieved a 100-rupee note from his pocket, pressing it into Chottu's hand. Chottu hesitated briefly before accepting the money with a nod of gratitude.

Sensing the chance to uncover the truth, Manoj and I stood and made our way toward the boy. The restaurant, sparsely occupied, seemed to heighten the intensity of the moment. The boy's posture stiffened as we approached, his annoyance giving way to a defensive edge.

"What do you want?" he asked, his voice carrying a mixture of suspicion and defiance.

"Don't be alarmed," I began, offering a disarming tone. "We're here to find Rahul. We need to talk to him."

"What's this about?" he questioned, simultaneously reaching for his phone and dialing.

"It concerns someone he might have helped," I explained. Before I could elaborate, the boy spoke into the phone, his words laced with urgency. "Get in here fast. Something feels off."

"Wait," I said quickly, trying to calm the escalating situation. "It's not what you think. We're just looking for someone named Jannat—someone Rahul might have helped."

The arrival of another group interrupted the exchange. A young man, his presence commanding, strode in with three others close behind.

"What's going on?" he asked, his tone assertive.

"These guys are asking for you, Rahul," the boy explained, gesturing toward us. "They're looking for someone you may have helped. I wasn't sure what they wanted, so I thought it best to call you."

Chottu, ever watchful, interjected. "Saab ji, why don't you take this conversation outside? The owner will be back soon, and I don't want trouble here."

Rahul considered Chottu's suggestion, nodding in agreement. "Let's go outside," he said, leading the group as they surrounded Manoj and me, escorting us out.

The cool night air wrapped around us as we stepped into the dimly lit street. I turned to Rahul, offering a more formal introduction. "Hi, Rahul. My name is Dinesh, and this is Manoj."

Rahul's stance relaxed slightly, though his skepticism lingered. "Hi," he replied, his accent polished. "What's this about? Make it quick—it's late."

"We're looking for someone named Jannat," I said, getting straight to the point. "She worked here, and we believe you helped her."

The name landed like a heavy stone, sending ripples through the group. The weight of it silenced them momentarily, the tension palpable as they processed the unexpected mention.

"What about her?" Rahul asked, his composure faltering just enough to reveal a flicker of unease.

Sensing his apprehension, I spoke quickly. "I mean no harm. I just want to know if she's okay. I've been searching for her for a long time, and every lead has brought me closer but never close enough."

Rahul's eyes narrowed, his wariness resurfacing. "And why should I trust you?"

"I don't expect blind trust," I replied, my voice steady. "But you can check my story. I'm not here to take her away or disrupt her life. I just need to know she's safe. That's all."

Rahul's friends exchanged uneasy glances, their restlessness growing. "Look," he finally said, "give me your number. I'll get back to you. This is not the place or the time to discuss this matter."

I found the opportunity slipping away from me.

I punched in my number on his phone, sensing the conversation was nearing its end. "Thank you," I said earnestly. "I hope you'll reach out."

The group turned to leave, their departure punctuated by the low rumble of the BMW's engine. As the car disappeared into the night, Manoj voiced his doubts. "Do you think he will call?"

"I don't know," I admitted. "But I had to try. There was nothing else I could do."

As we swiftly got into the car and left the area, I caught the sight of Saleem coming in the opposite direction. His menacing bearded face behind the steering wheel was hard to miss even at night. As our cars passed each other in opposite directions, in that brief moment, I caught a glimpse of someone seated in Saleem's car—a familiar figure whose presence sent a chill down my spine.

My mind raced to comprehend what my eyes had just witnessed. Was it her with Saleem? And what connection did she have to the unfolding events of the night?

Manoj was talking but I was not listening to him. The fleeting glimpse of the mysterious figure in Saleem's car remained etched in my memory.

"It can't be true," I kept telling myself. "I must be imagining things." However, doubt lingered, and a surge of urgency overcame me.

"Hold on, Manoj. Turn the car," I instructed, my voice carrying a sense of urgency.

Manoj screeched the car to a halt, a puzzled expression on his face. "What happened?"

"Just do as I'm telling you. We don't have any time to lose. Quick, turn the car towards Saleem's restaurant."

"You want to talk to Saleem at this godforsaken hour?" Manoj questioned as he reluctantly turned the car in the opposite direction. "He's just returning from a place where a murder has taken place, and you want to speak to him. Have you gone nuts?"

"Just do it, Manoj, and pull a little distance away. I don't want him to see us," I replied, my mind focused on confirming what my eyes had seen. The urgency in my voice left no room for further questioning.

Within minutes, we were parked at a discreet distance from Saleem's car as it pulled outside Saleem's restaurant. I anxiously observed as the driver's side door of Saleem's car opened, and he stepped out. Moments later, he opened the rear door, and a figure emerged – a figure my eyes recognized, but my mind struggled to acknowledge.

Looking visibly scared, fear etched on her face, she glanced at Saleem as he gestured towards the first floor of the building where the restaurant was located. He led the way, and she followed, disappearing from my view. I kept my eyes glued to the rearview mirror until she was completely out of sight.

"She's with him," I whispered, my voice trembling with disbelief.

"What? Who?" Manoj asked, alarmed.

"Nilofer," I replied, my pulse quickening. "She's with Saleem."

The realization struck like a lightning bolt, igniting a flurry of thoughts and questions. Why was she there? What was her connection to Saleem?

The night had taken an unexpected turn, plunging us deeper into a web of mystery and danger. What awaited us in the near future was uncertain, but one thing was clear—this story was far from over.

Chapter 32

The revelation hit us like a thunderbolt, sending shockwaves through our already frazzled nerves. Nilofer, the enigmatic figure linked to Jannat's disappearance, was here at Saleem's restaurant in the dead of night—an unexpected twist in the tangled web of secrets and deceit that had ensnared us all.

Questions swirled in my mind like a whirlwind, each one more urgent than the last. What was Nilofer doing here? What connection did she have to Saleem, and to the events that had brought us to this moment? And most importantly, what did she know about Jannat's disappearance that she wasn't telling us?

Chottu was awake when Nilofer had been brought into the house by Saleem on the night that Sadiq, the paanwallah, had been murdered. That was three weeks ago. Saleem was walking ahead, and a petite girl, no older than 18, maybe 17, was following him. Her eyes rested on his, and Chottu had smiled. She had not returned the smile.

"Chottu, this is Nilofer, your sister. Take care of her and do not let anything go wrong this time," Saleem said, making sure that Chottu understood the relevance of the word this and making an obvious reference to the time that Jannat escaped.

"Jee," he replied.

"Now Nilofer, beta," Saleem was talking to Nilofer. "Do not worry about anything. Please treat this as your own house. Chottu here will take care of all your needs. Try to forget what happened. What happened to your father is unfortunate."

Not unfortunate at all, thought Nilofer.

"You settle down, rest, and we can chat in the morning."

"What about Aman? What will happen to him now?"

"Oh, he will be arrested but will be transferred to a juvenile center. These court cases get dragged on forever, but usually, in the case of juveniles, they need to spend a year in the juvenile center, after which time they will be released without a charge. Remember the Nirbhaya case? That is exactly what happened there and what will happen in this case too. He will agree to take full responsibility for the murder as he is a juvenile and can get away with a minimum sentence. You, on the other hand, would have had to spend a lifetime, and what good is that to anybody? This way, he will be out in a year or so, and you will be there to take care of him thereon. Does that not make sense?"

Nilofer had to silently agree that it did make sense in a convoluted way.

Chottu looked at Nilofer as the conversation unfolded and could not help but find a similarity with how Jannat's story had unfolded. She had been brought in with the same narrative of care and love.

"C'mon. Take her upstairs," ordered Saleem with a look in Chottu's direction. So, saying, he asked her to go up the stairs leading to the first floor and motioned Chottu to join.

"Where is Jannat?" Nilofer asked as she walked towards the stairs.

"Oh, she is not here today. She had to go to my wife's house and will be staying there for a week or so. Don't worry. She will be back here soon. I have already told her that you are here, and she is excited." Saleem smiled, but Nilofer did not return his smile.

Nilofer's worry began to intensify, caught between returning to the scene of the murder and an uncertain future with the police and society or continuing with a sense, however misplaced, of certainty in Saleem's household. She felt caught in two worlds—one she needed to survive and the other she needed to live—both equally uncertain now.

"Let's go," it was Chottu, the only person who seemed genuine.

As they reached the room, Chottu gestured towards it, his silence speaking volumes as Nilofer's mind raced with a whirlwind of emotions and questions. The events of the night flashed before her eyes like a vivid nightmare—the glint of the knife, the spatter of blood, and the sight of Aman, alias Chottu, caught amid danger.

Questions haunted her every thought, each one more pressing than the last. How was Aman? Had he come to any harm in her absence? And most importantly, had she done the right thing by leaving him alone with the wolves—the dangerous figures that lurked in the shadows of G.B. Road?

The weight of guilt settled heavily on her shoulders as she grappled with the uncertainty of the situation. Aman couldn't even speak, couldn't defend himself against the dangers that surrounded him. What was happening to him now, alone in that room with no one to protect him?

The fear of the unknown gnawed at Nilofer's heart, filling her with a sense of helplessness that threatened to consume her. Amidst the darkness, a glimmer of determination flickered, a resolve to find answers, to ensure Aman's safety, and to uncover the truth behind the mysteries that had brought them to this moment.

As she stepped into the room, her resolve burning bright, she knew that the journey ahead would test her in ways she could scarcely imagine. For Aman's sake, and for the sake of all those who had been wronged, she would not falter.

"If you need anything, then let me know. I sleep downstairs by the kitchen," Chottu said, trying to be reassuring.

Nilofer broke the silence and spoke for the first time that night. Her words, laden with a mixture of vulnerability and determination, echoed in the stillness of the room. Her voice broke through the heavy tension that had gripped the air. Chottu turned to her, their eyes reflecting a curious blend of surprise and anticipation. The room seemed to hold its breath, waiting for her to reveal the thoughts and emotions she had kept hidden.

"Chottu, is it true what Saleem's uncle said about Jannat?" Nilofer finally spoke up.

Chottu did not respond, hastily making his way back to the ground floor. He dusted the floor and lay down, his mind racing with the events of the crazy night. As he lay on the floor, his mind replayed the events of the night. He had been entrusted with a responsibility, a duty to take care of Nilofer, Saleem's latest addition to the household. It had been a night of uncertainty, questions, and the weight of secrets.

As he lay there, his mind wandered into the maze of possibilities that this night had opened up for him. The prospect of a good incentive fueled his imagination. Thoughts of what he could do with the extra money raced through his mind. Perhaps he could send some money back to his family, providing them with a reprieve from their financial struggles. Maybe he could help his ailing parents with medical expenses. The possibilities seemed endless, and the anticipation of a better future fueled a glimmer of hope in his heart, perhaps at any cost.

Chottu also couldn't help but wonder about the complexities of the situation. Nilofer's arrival echoed the past, a déjà vu of the time when Jannat had entered Saleem's household under similar circumstances. The parallel between the two stories raised questions, but Chottu dared not voice them.

The night had been crazy, and the air was thick with unspoken fears and uncertainties. He couldn't shake off the nagging thoughts about Jannat and the truth behind Saleem's words.

Nilofer, on the other hand, found herself caught in a difficult situation. The promise of a secure environment at Saleem's house contrasted sharply with the haunting images of the murder scene. The knife, the blood, and the lingering question of whether she had made the right choice loomed over her.

In her new room, Nilofer's mind raced with worry about Aman. How was he coping with the aftermath? Was he safe? Guilt gnawed at her, questioning the decision to leave him behind.

Chottu, aware of Nilofer's concerns, hesitated to respond to her query about Jannat. The truth hung in the air, unspoken but palpable. The night had woven a web of secrecy, and Chottu, caught in its intricate threads, could only hope that the incentives promised to him would outweigh the burdens of the clandestine world he found himself entangled in.

He realized that the path ahead was uncertain, and the choices made tonight would ripple through the lives of those involved. The night had brought rewards, but it also left a lingering sense of unease in the air, as if the consequences of their actions were shadows waiting to emerge from the darkness.

The Future

Chapter 33

"Salaam Aliekum Saleem miyan. How are you? It has been a long time since we last spoke. Is everything ok?"

"Aleikum Salaam. Everything is fine," replied Saleem. "Things have been a bit rough of late. Over the past months, Jannat ran away with some person, I do not know who, and now just some weeks back Sadiq got murdered."

"Yes, I heard. How did it happen?" inquired Roopak the pimp.

"He had got this boy from somewhere and he used to help out at his paan shop and also at home. You may have seen him. The boy who could not speak."

"Yes, yes."

"The bastard. He freaking slit Sadiq bhai's throat, just killed him! The man who rescued him from the streets gave him a home, food, and work – gone, murdered by that boy. These people have zero gratitude. You know how close I was with Sadiq, right? So, one of the neighbors calls me up and tells me to get to the house urgently. I rush in, and there he is, Sadiq, lying in a damn pool of blood, a freaking gash on his neck, blood splattered all over." Saleem paused to gather his breath and get control of his rising emotions.

"You know what ticks me off even more?" Saleem continued " That wretch is just sitting on the sofa, staring at the body. Can you believe it? Sadiq was like a guardian angel to him, and this is how he repays it. It's messed up, man. The whole thing – the violence, the betrayal – it's just too much to handle. So damn frustrating!"

"That's awful. So what happened to the boy?" asked Roopak unable to contain his impatience.

"I don't know. He will be, most likely, be taken away by the police officers who were on the way but I had left by then. I did not want to stay a moment longer."

There was a pause at the other end and Saleem failed to understand why Roopak had muted the call.

"Sorry." Roopak had unmuted the call "I accidentally pressed the mute button. What about Nilofer? What are your plans for her?"

"I managed to convince her to come with me. She did not want to but I had to stress that the boy had committed murder and there was nothing she could do. The good news was that the boy would be out in a year since he was a juvenile. After much persuasion, she decided to come with me. I told her that she would be safe with Jannat."

"Well played.' Roopak said 'You are a pro at this. Now what is the plan? Anything on your mind."

"Business has to go on.' Saleem continued. 'There is no time fretting over what has already transpired. Do you want to solicit a buyer for Nilofer? From all that I know about her, she should fetch a good price.'

There was a long silence at the other end. The call had been muted again.

"Hello, are you there?"

"Sorry bhai. I was thinking. Yes, yes. That should not be a problem at all. You tell me when you would like to meet and we can settle the terms."

Saleem was beginning to get uncomfortable with the pauses in the conversation.

"I would like to do that as soon as possible since the police officers may start by looking for her. I can always say that I took her under my wing as she was scared and inconsolable. Bringing her to my house was the only option. Then I can simply file a missing person's report, pay a few guys off, and rest in peace."

"You seem to have thought of everything you son of a bitch." guffawed Roopak.

"Ok, let's plan to meet then. I will let you know."

"Yes, let me get back to you after speaking to Neerja bi." The phone line went dead.

Saleem leaned back in his chair, the weight of the conversation with Roopak pressing down on him like a vice. The unease from the call now grew into a gnawing suspicion, tugging at the edges of his composure. Nilofer's name lingered in his mind. The way Roopak had responded sparked a series of questions that refused to be silenced.

He replayed the exchange in his head, his brow furrowing as he tried to pinpoint the exact moment when the conversation had taken a turn. Roopak's pauses, his muted responses, and those seemingly casual remarks—each detail now stood out as a potential clue, a thread in the web of deceit Saleem had spun around himself.

"How did he know about her?" Saleem muttered, his voice low but heavy with doubt. The question gnawed at him, unraveling the confidence he'd carried moments before. He reached for his glass of whisky, the liquid swirling as his hand trembled ever so slightly. Taking a long sip, he let the burn settle his nerves, but it did little to quiet his racing thoughts.

The room felt suffocating, its dark curtains and muted tones amplifying the tension in the air. Saleem's gaze darted to the phone on the table. The device that had carried the conversation now seemed like a conduit for betrayal. Shadows cast by the dim light seemed to move of their own accord, mocking his faltering sense of control.

He needed clarity. Picking up the phone, he dialed Neerja Bi, the woman who had been a linchpin in his operations for years. Her calm demeanor and sharp instincts had always been a source of stability in his volatile world. The phone rang, each tone echoing the uncertainty that gripped him.

"Saleem Bhai, how may I assist you today?" Neerja's voice came through, steady and composed, a stark contrast to the chaos in Saleem's mind. "I heard the news. A lot seems to be happening around you, doesn't it? Is that why you've remembered me?"

"Neerja bi," Saleem began, his tone measured but insistent. "I've got something to discuss with you. Do you know anything about a new girl I've got ready to initiate into your world? Her name is Nilofer."

The pause on the other end was deafening. Saleem held his breath, the seconds stretching into what felt like an eternity. When Neerja finally spoke, her voice was steady but carried an undercurrent of curiosity.

"Saleem Bhai, I've no idea who this Nilofer is. This is the first time I've heard her name. What's her story?"

Saleem exhaled slowly, the tension in his chest easing slightly, but not disappearing entirely. "She's new stock I've recently acquired. I wanted to ensure you were the first to know about her."

"Well, that's considerate of you," Neerja replied, her tone cool and businesslike. "Let me know if there's anything else I can do to assist. Let's settle the deal quickly, though. There's a lot of visibility on you lately. I've got some excellent buyers lined up, and they'll pay handsomely, but we can't waste time."

The call ended, leaving Saleem in a state of uneasy relief. While Neerja's words had provided some reassurance, the doubt planted by Roopak's behavior remained. Saleem placed the phone back on the table, his mind still racing with possibilities.

The shadows in the room seemed to close in around him as he considered his next move. Trust, already a rare commodity in his world, now felt like a luxury he could no longer afford. Saleem's thoughts turned to the intricate network of alliances and secrets he'd built over the years, each one now seeming like a potential vulnerability.

"How did Roopak get to know about Nilofer?" The question lingered, unanswered and insistent. Saleem realized the balance he'd worked so hard to maintain was precarious at best. The call with Roopak had not just unsettled him—it had cracked the foundation of his confidence, leaving him questioning everything and everyone.

As the night deepened, Saleem resolved to uncover the truth, no matter the cost. The stakes had never been higher, and the shadows that danced around him whispered of betrayals yet to come.

Chapter 34

As the days passed, Nilofer found herself grappling with an unsettling sense of uncertainty about her future in Saleem's household. At first, her treatment seemed amicable; she was tasked with chores like chopping vegetables, cleaning the kitchen, and helping out around the restaurant. Chottu, who appeared to be both the caretaker and Saleem's trusted right-hand, was eager to assist her.

Despite Chottu's outward friendliness and the way he affectionately referred to her as "his sister," Nilofer couldn't shake the feeling that something about him was off. His overly enthusiastic gestures of support left her suspicious as if motives were lurking beneath his helpful facade.

One evening, after an exhausting day preparing for a large dinner party of 20, Chottu remarked, "You must be knackered."

Wiping her brow with her dupatta, Nilofer responded curtly, "I'm fine." The air between them carried an unspoken tension, the kind that made every exchange feel charged with hidden implications.

Chottu leaned on the counter, watching her carefully. "You work fast. Were you made to work this hard at Sadiq's house too?"

Nilofer's tone sharpened as she replied, "Not really. I was with family there. His daughter." Her voice faltered slightly, aware of her deliberate use of the past tense. "I helped out like anyone in the family would. Most of my time was spent with Aman—he was like the younger brother I never had. It wasn't easy, though."

"What do you mean?" Chottu asked, his curiosity piqued.

"Abba wasn't exactly father of the year," she said bitterly. "He was a tyrant. Every day, I grew to despise him more. As his daughter, I suffered enough, but Aman… Aman had it worse. The way Abba treated him—physically, and verbally—broke me. I'd cry watching him endure it, but what could I do? Aman couldn't even defend himself. He could barely speak, let alone stand up to Abba."

Chottu hesitated. "And Aman… did he…?"

"Yes," Nilofer interrupted, her voice laced with quiet pride. "He did what needed to be done. Abba deserved what he got. I'd wanted to do it myself more times than I can count, but I couldn't bring myself to. For Aman, it was just a matter of time." She paused, her voice softening. "Pass me the coriander, Chottu."

He fetched the coriander from across the kitchen and handed it to her, his expression unreadable. "Were you there when it happened?"

"You've asked me that a dozen times already," she snapped. "I don't want to talk about it."

"Well, maybe you'd answer if you'd just told me the first time," Chottu shot back, his tone defensive.

Nilofer sighed, her patience wearing thin. "Fine. I was in the kitchen, looking for a knife to cut onions. I couldn't find it because Aman had already taken it. He'd made up his mind. I heard Abba shouting at him—same old insults, the same fury. Then, mid-sentence, he stopped. All I heard after that was this guttural choking sound and the crash of a glass hitting the floor.

"I ran out and saw him, Abba clutching his neck, blood pouring everywhere. Aman was behind him, gripping his hair with one hand and the knife in the other. It was over in seconds. Abba slumped onto the sofa, and it just… turned red."

"Oh my God," Chottu muttered, the color draining from his face. "Why didn't you run? Why didn't you try to escape?"

"And go where?" Nilofer replied, her voice heavy with frustration. "Aman and I wouldn't have lasted a day on the streets. We had no one. I told Aman to wait for the police and go with them. He's a juvenile. He'll get a year in detention and then walk free. As for me, Saleem showed up that very night and told me to come with him. I didn't want to, but I didn't have a choice. At least I'd be alive. I thought I could wait here until Aman was released, and…" She trailed off, her voice thick with emotion.

"And you thought you'd find Jannat here," Chottu finished for her, his voice low.

"I didn't know any better then. Saleem fooled me into believing she was here," Nilofer admitted, a hint of regret seeping into her words. She sprinkled the fresh coriander over the salad with a grace that contrasted starkly with the heaviness of her tone.

Chottu nodded solemnly. "Jannat didn't stay long. She ran off with some boys. Saleem didn't bother looking for her. Said she was more trouble than she was worth. He was happy to see her go."

Nilofer froze for a moment, the weight of Chottu's words settling over her. The Jannat she had thought of as a sister, the one she had hoped to find solace in, had taken a path so far removed from what Nilofer had imagined. But there was no time to dwell on the loss—guests were arriving, and the kitchen's atmosphere shifted with the din of laughter and chatter.

Forcing a smile, Nilofer returned to her work, concealing the turmoil within her. The contrast between the bustling energy of the dinner preparations and the somber truths she had just uncovered created a dissonance only she could truly feel.

Chapter 35

The relentless passage of time amplified the void left by Rahul's silence. Sleepless nights were consumed by questions echoing endlessly in my mind. It became clear that Rahul was likely bound by familial constraints, perhaps firmly instructed not to reveal anything about Jannat. His visits to Saleem's restaurant grew infrequent, each absence chipping away at the fragile hope I clung to.

Without contact details, reaching Rahul felt impossible. My efforts to bridge the gap were futile, and the ever-growing uncertainty cast a shadow over my optimism. I wandered through a labyrinth of possibilities, grappling with why Rahul remained silent and the power his family might wield over him.

Visits to Saleem's restaurant became bittersweet rituals. Each inquiry about Rahul felt like walking a tightrope under Saleem's watchful gaze. Chottu caught between loyalty and survival, bore the brunt of unspoken tensions. The memory of his punishment after aiding Jannat's escape lingered like a warning.

Chottu's guarded demeanor revealed the toll of these internal battles. His once-eager gestures had turned cautious, his every move calculated. The restaurant, once a place of camaraderie, now carried an undercurrent of secrecy and suppressed emotions.

Weeks turned into months, and the restaurant's unease mirrored my turmoil. The unanswered questions about Jannat and Rahul's silence became haunting presences, constant reminders of the mysteries that refused to unravel. Caught in a sea of uncertainty, I found myself battling between hope and despair, unsure when—or if—answers would ever surface.

"Is Nilofer here?" My simple question shattered the fragile peace of the restaurant. Saleem, overhearing, erupted with fury. In a heartbeat, I was forcibly ejected, the door slamming behind me with a resounding finality.

The fallout didn't end there. Saleem's anger turned on Chottu, whose loyalty had become a liability. The slap that echoed through the restaurant wasn't just physical; it severed trust and created an irreversible rift.

Chottu, stunned and bleeding from the nose, bore the brunt of Saleem's wrath. The pain etched across his face mirrored the broken remnants of my tenuous connection to this place. At that moment, any hope of rekindling conversations with Chottu—or reaching Nilofer—crumbled into nothing.

Saleem's restaurant was no longer a place of refuge but a realm of closed doors and unwelcome memories. The abrupt expulsion drew a line between me and the answers I desperately sought. I was left to navigate the maze of uncertainties alone, wounded in ways that extended far beyond the physical.

It was then that I conceived a final plan—a plan so audacious, it just might work.

When I met Manoj a couple of days later, I recounted what had happened at the restaurant. He laughed at my recklessness. "What were you thinking, walking in and asking about someone who disappeared under the shadiest circumstances?"

"I wasn't," I admitted, starting to realize the depth of my stupidity.

Still, when I explained my plan, he listened with interest. "It's dangerous," he said, leaning back, "but it might work—if you play it right. That guy only cares about money, but would he sell out his people?"

"If the price is right," I replied, "he'd sell his mother."

Manoj nodded. "True."

The journey to meet our contact was uneventful, but the tension was palpable. As we arrived, it was easy to spot him, surrounded by his cronies, laughing loudly and punctuating every joke with colorful expletives.

When he saw us, his grin widened. "Arre, you're back," he jeered. "What's the rush this time? Can't keep it in your pants, can you?" His laughter erupted, revealing teeth stained red from betel and tobacco.

Ignoring his taunts, I got straight to the point. "We have a job for you."

The mood shifted. His grin faded as he recognized the seriousness in my tone. The crude banter gave way to an air of businesslike professionalism.

"I know the man," he said after hearing us out. "Talking to him won't be a problem. Consider it done. But how much are you offering?"

"Five thousand," I said firmly.

"Five thousand?" He spat on the ground. "Get lost. Ten, and no bargaining."

Reluctantly, we agreed.

I handed over the money, and he counted it with practiced precision before saluting theatrically. He then melted back into his group, the boisterous laughter resuming as if we'd never been there.

A knot of unease tightened in my stomach as we watched him retreat. Had I made the right choice?

Once the call to Saleem was made and I received the answers I sought, doubt crept in. I confided in Manoj. "I shouldn't have had him ask that one question."

"Which one?" Manoj asked, his concern evident.

"When I told him to ask Saleem how Nilofer was," I admitted, the apprehension in my voice undeniable. That single question now loomed large in my mind, a potential crack in the delicate web of secrecy we'd constructed. As we drove into the night, I couldn't help but wonder if that slip might cost us everything.

Chapter 36

The weight of the situation bore down on me like an unrelenting storm cloud. Nilofer's fate teetered on the edge of a precipice, poised to plunge into the very darkness I had vowed to save her from. The turbulence of emotions, combined with unforeseen complications, left me feeling increasingly helpless, as though the world were closing in.

The need to warn Nilofer burned within me, but every path forward seemed blocked by invisible barriers. Saleem's restaurant had become an impenetrable fortress, guarded by his ever-watchful gaze. Any attempt to approach risked disaster, and the clock ticked away relentlessly, mocking my inaction.

Doubt crept into my resolve like a persistent whisper, urging me to walk away. You can't fix this. You're just making things worse. But I had come too far to retreat now. I couldn't let fear or failure dictate my choices, not when Nilofer's life hung in the balance.

The shadow of despair grew darker with each passing day, but even amidst the chaos, I clung to a flicker of determination. If I had learned anything, it was that standing at the crossroads of courage and defeat demanded more than conviction—it demanded action.

I called Manoj. He had been my steady ally through every twist and turn, despite the toll it had taken on him. His patience had been tested time and again, yet here he was, still willing to listen.

"So now it's Nilofer," Manoj said, his tone tinged with exasperation. "I get that you want to help her, but don't you see how this is spiraling out of control? We're peeling layer after layer, and it's not just tears we're dealing with—it's danger."

He had a point, but I couldn't let go. "At least let me warn her," I pleaded. "She deserves to know what's coming. I can't just stand by knowing what Saleem has planned for her."

"And how do you plan to do that?" Manoj challenged. "Saleem would have you chopped into pieces if you so much as set foot near that place again. You can't reach Nilofer, so what's your plan?"

I paused, frustrated. Then, like a lightbulb flickering to life, the answer hit me. "Chottu."

Manoj raised an eyebrow. "How do you reach him?"

"The phone," I realized. "The flip phone I gave him! He still has it—he must!"

Late that night, I sent a text. It was the only way to reach Chottu without risking his safety—or mine. "Can you talk, Chottu? This is Dinesh—the same Dinesh who came to the restaurant looking for Rahul. Remember?"

Minutes stretched into what felt like hours. Doubt gnawed at me. What if Saleem confiscated the phone? Then, finally, the reply came.

"Yes, I'm here. We can't talk, but we can text."

Relief flooded over me, tempered by the urgency of the situation. "Need to speak urgently. When can I call?"

"Wait. Let me go downstairs to the restaurant. Saleem is asleep in the other room," came the reply.

I held my breath as I imagined Chottu creeping downstairs, every step laden with risk. Then the phone buzzed again. "Yes, I'm here."

"Chottu, are you okay?" I asked.

"Yes. I didn't call you because I had no updates. The boys never came back. But I have something to tell you."

My heart raced. "What is it?"

"Saleem brought a girl here. Her name is Nilofer. She knows Jannat but doesn't know where she is now. He's tricked her into thinking Jannat is staying at his wife's house. But we both know that's a lie—there is no wife, no house."

The line went quiet for a moment, then Chottu continued. "What's going on? What do you need from me?"

"Chottu, listen carefully," I said. "Nilofer's life is in danger. Saleem plans to sell her to a pimp on G.B. Road. We must get her out of there before it's too late."

"How do you know this?" Chottu asked, suspicion creeping into his voice.

"I paid someone to gather information," I admitted. "There's no time to explain. Please, Chottu, warn Nilofer. Help her escape before it's too late."

There was silence. "Chottu, are you there?" I asked, panic creeping in.

"Yes, Saab," he replied finally. "I'll do what I can."

"Good," I said. "Let me kno—" The line went dead.

My stomach sank. What if Saleem overheard? The silence stretched into an unbearable void. I paced the room, the minutes dragging into eternity. Then, the phone rang again.

"Sorry, the battery died," Chottu explained. "I had to charge it secretly. I can't do it during the day—Saleem would find out."

"Listen," I said urgently. "Saleem's plans are moving quickly. You have to act now."

"I will, Saab," Chottu replied. The line clicked off again.

This time, I knew there would be no callback.

"Good," Chottu said, his voice steady as he turned to Saleem. "There's no proof."

"Excellent," Saleem replied with a cold smile. "You've done well. Two can play this game."

Chottu grinned, the weight of betrayal lightened by the promise of a reward. His parents would be taken care of now, and that was all that mattered to him.

For Nilofer, the storm was just beginning.

Chapter 37

Jannat found herself ensnared in an intricate web of despair and control within Saleem's household. At first, there was a pretense of kindness—a hollow, brittle facade. By day, she toiled in the kitchen, her hands busy with tasks that grounded her in the monotony of survival. By night, she was plunged into the abyss of Saleem's vile desires, a victim of a man who should have been her protector. The oppressive air within the house grew heavier with each passing moment, and though Chottu bore silent witness to her plight, fear kept him rooted to the sidelines.

The atmosphere inside Saleem's restaurant cum house was steeped in fear. Saleem's vast network of connections made the idea of escape feel futile. Chottu, bound by the weight of duty to his aging parents and young siblings, found himself cornered. His job, with all its darkness, was the lifeline keeping his family afloat in their village. Medical bills, marriage costs, and the endless cycle of need pressed on him with suffocating urgency.

The lines between right and wrong blurred for Chottu as the harsh realities of life forced him to compromise. He grappled with the moral balance of his choices. Every action weighed against the promise of a better life for his family, and in that battle, the morally ambiguous path often won.

Jannat, however, remained resilient. Despite the crushing experiences of her life, a quiet fire burned within her, refusing to be extinguished. That fire caught Rahul's attention. Their fateful meeting marked a moment of unexpected possibility in her bleak world, a glimmer of hope that maybe, just maybe, she could dream again.

"Not seen you before. Are you new here?" Rahul asked as Jannat wiped the table for his group's dinner order.

"Yes, bhaiyya," she replied, avoiding his gaze. "I'm new here."

"A relative of Saleem bhai?"

"No, more of a victim," she said flatly. "He bought me from a paanwallah. I've been here ever since."

Rahul's face darkened with shock. As Jannat turned to leave, he stopped her. "Why don't you leave? Try your luck somewhere else."

She hesitated, glancing around nervously. "People like me have no choice, bhaiyya. If I say anything against him, his men will burn me alive. The police are on his payroll. Chottu is the only one I think I can trust, but even with him, I'm not sure."

"I can help."

"Please don't, bhaiyya," she whispered, her voice taut with fear. "If Saleem sees us talking, I'll never leave my room again. Not on my own two feet."

Rahul watched her walk away, her words weighing heavily on his conscience. He turned to his friends, his expression grim.

"What do you think, guys?" he asked.

"You have to do something," one of his friends said firmly. "You have the resources. Use them."

Rahul shook his head. "Talking to Saleem won't help. He'll make sure there's no trace of her by morning."

Three days later, they returned. This time, Rahul was determined.

"Where's the girl?" he asked Chottu as soon as they were seated.

"Which one, Saab?" Chottu replied cautiously.

"You know who I mean. Don't play dumb. I'll make it worth your while."

Chottu's eyes flickered with recognition and calculation. The incentives Rahul offered were a lifeline for Chottu's family, a chance to ease their burdens, if only temporarily.

"I'll bring her, but don't make it obvious," Chottu whispered, tipping over a jar of water. The liquid spilled across the table and onto the floor. "Sorry, saab. I'll send someone to clean it."

Jannat appeared minutes later, a mop in hand. She glanced briefly at Rahul but said nothing.

"Do you want to get out of here?" Rahul asked bluntly.

Jannat froze, then nodded. "Yes, saab. I've lived this life too long. I can't take it anymore."

"I can help you."

"How can I trust you, saab?"

"You can't," he admitted. "But you must believe me. That's all I can offer."

Her shoulders sagged. "I've nothing left to lose. My life can't possibly get worse."

Rahul winced at the stark truth of her words. He made her a promise then, a silent vow to give her the freedom she deserved.

In the days that followed, Rahul's friends became messengers, passing notes through Chottu. For Chottu, the small rewards he received were vital. For Jannat, they were lifelines of hope.

Finally, the day arrived. In the dead of night, Chottu led Jannat out of the restaurant. Waiting for her was an elderly couple—Rahul's parents. Without hesitation, she climbed into their car, pausing only to wave goodbye to Chottu.

That night, Chottu cried like a child. For the first time in his life, he felt he had done something truly right. Yet, as dawn approached, fear gripped him. He had defied Saleem. He had done the unthinkable.

The next morning, Chottu braced himself for the fallout. This, he knew, would be the last good thing he ever did.

In the labyrinth of deceit and oppression that was Saleem's world, Chottu's small act of defiance stood as a fragile beacon of hope. The lines of loyalty and morality had never been so blurred, but in that fleeting moment, he chose humanity over fear, knowing full well the price he might have to pay.

Chapter 38

Aman, his face shadowed with a mix of fear and resignation, was led away to judicial custody, marking the start of a turbulent legal journey. Efforts to locate his so-called sister, Nilofer, had proven fruitless, cloaking the entire case in a haze of mystery. The police, relentless in their pursuit of the truth, made their way to Saleem—the man whose enigmatic presence loomed large over the unfolding drama.

Saleem, ever the slippery figure, met their questions with a practiced charm. Producing a meticulously crafted missing person report, he managed to paint himself as a concerned and cooperative citizen. The document, displayed with precision, served as a shield, keeping any immediate suspicion at bay. Though the officers harbored doubts, they found themselves temporarily stalled, unable to tie Saleem directly to the allegations.

The missing person report became a pivotal piece of evidence, casting Saleem in a favorable light. For now, it worked. The police, momentarily swayed by the appearance of compliance, had no choice but to retreat and recalibrate their approach.

As the officers escorted Aman to the waiting police jeep, his eyes met mine, desperate and pleading, though his lips remained silent. I stepped closer, fighting the weight of helplessness that threatened to pull me under.

"I'll be waiting for you when you return," I shouted, my voice cutting through the din of the courthouse.

For a brief moment, his face softened into a smile—perhaps the first genuine one I had ever seen from him. It was a fleeting glimpse of hope as he climbed into the jeep, the door slamming shut behind him.

I stood there, rooted to the spot until the jeep disappeared from view. Returning to my car, my phone buzzed insistently in my pocket. Assuming it was yet another credit card sales pitch, I disconnected the call without a second thought. But the phone rang again, and again I dismissed it.

Moments later, a text lit up my screen.

"Please pick up. This is Rahul (Jannat)."

My heart leaped as I fumbled to call him back. He answered on the first ring.

"Rahul! I'm so sorry. I didn't recognize the number," I stammered.

"It's fine," he replied, his tone steady. "Listen, I have some good news. My parents have agreed to let you visit Jannat."

The words hit me like a thunderclap. For a moment, I couldn't speak, overwhelmed by a rush of relief and gratitude.

"We've been watching you for months now," Rahul continued. "We even did some background checks. Honestly, your visits to G.B. Road were a red flag. Care to explain?"

I recounted everything: the plan to gather evidence against Saleem, the use of Roopak as a decoy, and my desperate attempt to save Nilofer. My words carried the conviction of someone who had nothing to hide. Rahul listened intently.

"I know your father worked in the Ministry," he said after a pause. "A Cabinet Secretary, wasn't he? You come from a good family, which is why we're willing to trust you. Be at our place tomorrow by 3:30 p.m.

"Thank you, Rahul. I'll be there," I said, though the skepticism borne of so many false starts lingered in the back of my mind.

He ended the call abruptly, and within seconds, a text followed with the address:

A 2519, Netaji Nagar, Near Palika Bhawan.

The following day, I found myself seated on the lawn of a Type 5 flat in Netaji Nagar, Manoj by my side. Rahul's mother, a composed and dignified woman, greeted me warmly as tea was served.

"How is Jannat?" I asked, unable to mask the urgency in my voice.

"She's well," she replied. "Though I must tell you, she's now Riya. That was her idea when she came to us."

The transformation stunned me. Jannat—a name that had haunted me for years—was now Riya.

"Your work has saved a life," I said.

"We've merely given her hope," she corrected gently. "My husband and I run an NGO. For two decades, we've worked to provide better futures for underprivileged and exploited children. Riya is one of many. We've seen it all—broken spirits, shattered lives—but every child we help reminds us why we do this work. When Riya arrived, she bore deep emotional scars. It's taken months of therapy and care to help her begin healing."

As she spoke, I scanned the yard, my eyes searching for Jannat. But there was no sign of her.

"She's at school," Rahul's mother explained. "She's thriving, but healing is a slow process. Still, she's determined, and that determination is her strength."

Just as I began to accept that I might not see her, a figure appeared at the gate. Dressed in a pink-striped shirt and grey skirt, books in hand, she walked in with a quiet confidence that was both new and familiar.

"Hello, Mumma," she said, her voice sending a chill down my spine. It was Jannat.

I turned to face her fully, and for a moment, time seemed to stop. The haunted eyes and fearful demeanor I remembered were gone, replaced by a radiant calm. She glanced at me, just briefly, before turning to her mother with a bright smile.

"Hello," I managed to say, my voice barely audible.

"This is Riya," her mother said, introducing her as if to affirm her new identity.

"Hello," she replied, her gaze lingering on me for an extra second before she turned back to her mother, chatting animatedly about her day.

As she disappeared into the house, I felt an odd mix of emotions—relief that she was safe and thriving, but also a pang of sadness. She didn't seem to remember me, or perhaps she didn't want to.

Later, as Manoj and I prepared to leave, I caught a glimpse of her at the window. She dropped a slip of paper onto the windowsill before vanishing inside. Picking it up, my heart raced as I unfolded it.

"Bhaiyya, it's not that I didn't remember you. I just want to forget my past. Forgive me and thank you for everything. I will never forget you. I love you."

The car ride back was silent, the weight of her words settling over us. I shared the note with Manoj, who nodded in understanding but said nothing. For the first time in years, I felt an immense sense of closure.

Jannat—or Riya—was finally free, her life moving forward while mine remained forever marked by the journey to find her. It was a journey that had taken more than it gave, but in the end, it had been worth every step.

Chapter 39

As I stood in the now-familiar lanes, memories of the journey flooded back—each step, each obstacle, and each triumph etched vividly in my mind. The quest for the young girl had been long, fraught with challenges and moments of despair, yet it had succeeded. Her eyes were gleaming with a renewed light when she embraced the love of her new family. That moment had felt like the closing of a chapter.

Years had passed when curiosity tugged at me. I wanted to know yet again as to how she was doing. Was she happy? A part did not want to search for her anymore, tired as I was with the trials and tribulations that the last years had brought about. I had a family now and they required my undivided attention. Shayna had silently put up with my insensate desire to find closure and Manoj was not somebody I wanted to nudge again. I needed to close this once and for all.

I found myself sitting at the dining table one day, scrolling through my phone while Shayna and our daughter chatted about their day.

"Have you heard anything about her?" Shayna asked, her voice soft with curiosity as she poured tea. I looked up at her surprised.

"Jannat."

"That was random," I replied.

"It just struck me."

Not recently," I replied, though I had been meaning to check. "I've been wondering how she's doing. She seemed so happy the last time we saw her."

Our daughter looked up from her art project, her fingers smudged with paint.

"You should find out."

Encouraged by their words and needing no further prodding, I opened Facebook and searched for her name. The search for Riya revealed thousands of results, similar to another search I attempted under the name of Rahul. It was a hopeless exercise. I tried everything starting with the name, school, mutual connections, and further refining the search to medicine but to no avail.

Every day, I would spend time trying to search for the elusive Riya.

Then I saw it.

A name with no profile picture, just a name which read 'Riya Thanks you'. That was an odd one as I noticed that it was a private group. I sent a 'Join' request.

Some days later, I got the acceptance notification.

All interactive mediums had been disabled. The pictures told me the story I needed to know. Her new family had moved to the United States and the post showed her with Rahul standing in front of a suburban house with a white picket fence, their smiles wide and genuine. The once fragile demeanor had been replaced by an air of confidence and joy. She was holding a puppy in her arms, grinning ear to ear.

I stared at the screen for a long moment, processing the surge of emotions. I got overwhelmed but that was okay. She was exactly where she deserved to be.

"She looks so different," I murmured, tilting the screen toward Shayna who had joined me. "So confident. So... happy." Shayna leaned closer, a tender smile spreading across her face. "That's all because of you, you know. You gave her the chance to have this. Now, it's your turn to be happy.

Her words lingered as I reflected on the journey. The streets I had walked so many times were no longer tied to a purpose or a quest—they were just streets. The pressure of purpose that I had carried for so long was gone, replaced by a quiet, enduring peace.

As I tucked our daughter into bed that night, Shayna whispered in my ear, "Do you think she remembers you?"

I smiled, brushing a strand of hair from her face. "Maybe, but what matters is that she's happy."

For isn't that the beauty of life? Each ending, in its way, makes space for a new beginning.

EPILOGUE

"This cannot be true," I muttered, disbelief weighing down my voice. Manoj, catching my gaze, frowned in confusion.

"What are you talking about, dude?" he asked.

The scene unfolding before us was surreal, a stark contrast to the camaraderie we had shared earlier. The plan devised at my place with Abhay and Sunil had taken on a life of its own. While they had decided to push forward with a night out at Al Kauser and the final act of checking into a hotel with women of easy virtue, Manoj and I had opted out. We had drawn a line, content to let the evening end without venturing further.

In the hotel lobby, Manoj and I waited as Abhay and Sunil completed their check-in, their laughter echoing as they exchanged conspiratorial glances. We planned to leave soon, but fate had other ideas. As the entrance doors swung open, three women entered, their arrival shifting the air in the room. Manoj nudged me to look.

There they were: a trio of women —one in red, another in black, and a third in shorts. As they walked in, the girl in black led the way, her confident strides parting the lobby's quiet hum. But it was the girl in red who made the world tilt on its axis.

"Oh my god. This cannot be true," I whispered, my words barely audible, my breath catching in my throat. The familiarity of her face sent a jolt through me. "Oh my god. Isn't that…!"

Manoj froze, his eyes fixed on the girl in red. His face, usually composed, mirrored the shock I felt.

The realization hit us like a freight train. Standing before us, dressed in red and shrouded in circumstances we couldn't yet comprehend, was the very person we had been seeking, now caught in a scenario that defied everything we had hoped for her.

Nilofer.

Acknowledgements

My heartfelt gratitude goes to Ajay Mago, my publisher, for staying true to his belief in this project and for his trust in me. Your encouragement and support has greatly helped me realize my dream for the second time.

To Shantanu for always being available with your invaluable insights and guidance. Your perspective has enriched this work in many ways.

To Rhea for her meticulous editing and proofreading. Your dedication and sharp attention to detail have truly elevated this book to its finest form.

To the incredible team at Om Books International, I am deeply grateful for your tireless efforts in bringing this dream to life. Your collaboration and hard work have been instrumental in shaping Jannat's journey.

To all the characters in the book who shared this journey with me. Their presence in the book breathed life into the struggle that Dinesh faced and overcame. To the special friend who egged me on and ensured that I complete this journey no matter what the cost.

To Jannat, who will remain etched in my mind for years, and to this beautiful city of Delhi, which surprises everyone every day.

And finally to Nilofer who will remain an unexplained enigma but not for long!